Marguerite Bouvet

A child of Tuscany

Marguerite Bouvet

A child of Tuscany

ISBN/EAN: 9783337215408

Printed in Europe, USA, Canada, Australia, Japan

Cover: Foto ©Andreas Hilbeck / pixelio.de

More available books at **www.hansebooks.com**

BY

MARGUERITE BOUVET

AUTHOR OF "MY LADY," "SWEET WILLIAM," "LITTLE MARJORIE'S
LOVE STORY," "PRINCE TIP-TOP," ETC.

Illustrated by

WILL PHILLIPS HOOPER

CHICAGO
A. C. McCLURG AND COMPANY
1895

A CHILD of TUSCANY

By

MARGUERITE BOUVET

Illustrated by
Will Phillips Hooper

Chicago

A C McClurg & Co

MDCCCXCV

PREFACE.

I HOPE that you, my dear young readers, may some
day have the good fortune to know the quaint and
beautiful city where I have laid the scene of this little
story; for among all the cities of Europe there is none
more interesting, and which people learn to love better,
than Florence, — "Florence, the fairest and most famous
of the daughters of Rome!" as Dante calls her. You have
doubtless seen on your maps that Florence is situated
in the northern part of Italy. It is a city of noble
antiquity, having existed, some historians tell us, as early
as the Roman period. In the twelfth century it was
already the most important town of Tuscany, and after-
wards became the capital of the independent duchy of
that name; and there the princes and dukes held their
court. In 1861 all the provinces of Italy were united into
one kingdom under Victor Emmanuel, and the court was
removed to Rome, 1870. But Florence is still visited
every spring by many of the nobility of Europe, on account
of its delightful climate, its rich art galleries, and its many

interesting and beautiful old palaces. And I shall feel
happily repaid if anything I have said in this little vol-
ume has awakened in you an interest in the lovely city
and its charming people, and a desire to visit its many
treasures.

M. B.

Florence, May, 1894.

LIST OF ILLUSTRATIONS.

A CHILD OF TUSCANY.

CHAPTER I

AUSTINA and Raffaello lived alone in a small hut just beyond the village of Galluzzo; not quite alone, for there was Minnetto. Faustina was a very tall, dark-eyed, hard-faced woman; Raffaello was a small, curly-haired boy; and Minnetto was the cat, a Tuscan cat, with a beautiful coat of maltese gray, a monstrous head, and big sleepy eyes, and a long bushy tail that resembled the plumes on the Florentine soldiers' caps, whenever he encountered a neighboring dog. Raffaello and Minnetto were the best of friends;

they were about the same age and very nearly the same height. For, when Raffaello stood up near the table, of a morning, to eat his bread and milk, and Minnetto placed his two front paws on the little boy's shoulders, and stretched his long neck to get a sniff of the good breakfast, their two heads were almost on a level. As to Faustina, she was not a very genial companion; she never played with them, or fondled them, or called them by any loving names; but she took care of them both, gave them what she could to eat, and she was not unkind.

Minnetto did not mind this at all. He was happy if Raffaello let him lie in the warm sun, and did not stroke his fur the wrong way; and he would purr for hours with his head buried in the bend of Raffaello's little arm, and never seemed to find fault with his destiny. But not so with Raffaello. He often wondered how he and Faustina happened to be living in this lonely way together, who he was, and what he was, and why she was not his mother, and why he had no brothers and sisters like little Luigi yonder, at the village, but only Minnetto to play with, who was a good friend in his way, but only a cat after all, and who could not talk with him, or understand him when Raffaello tried to take him into his confidence. He had lived with Faus-

tina and the cat ever since he could remember anything, and Faustina had always grumbled, and the
cat had always blinked indifferently at her, and
Raffaello had always wondered at the strange little
family, and how he came to be a member of it.

There was one thing that puzzled Raffaello very
much. The other people in the village who were
poor lived in great stone houses that were old and
dismal, all huddled up together like a great many
bees in a very big hive; and all the children played
and romped together in the dingy courts, and set
up such a noise, that he and Faustina would often
hear them of a summer evening, as they sat upon
their stone steps; and the women would chat with
one another from their windows; and sometimes,
when any wandering musicians happened to be
passing through the town, everybody would flock
out into the streets, and dance, and dance till late in
the night,—young men and women, boys and girls, in
their quaint peasant's dress, whirling round and
round like gay windmills, while the old men sat on
boxes and barrels along the wall, smoking their
pipes, and enjoying the frolic as if they never
minded about being poor, and were all as happy as
people could be.

But with Faustina, Raffaello, and the cat, it was

very different. They never mingled with the simple, light-hearted, good-natured people at the village, or joined in any of their festivities. They lived in a very small hut of stone, which stood quite a distance down on the brow of the hill, and all the news they got of the doings of the people at Galluzzo was what the little streamlet brought, as it came laughing and tumbling down the rocky race to turn the big wheel of the mill hard by. Faustina never went to the village save to buy some necessary, like a bit of cloth, or a spool of thread, or a lace needle; for their wants were very few, and their purse was very slender. But they had their own goat, which supplied them with milk, and a bit of a garden on the sunny side of the hut, that gave them a few vegetables in the spring, and a little fruit in the summer, just enough for their own small needs. In the winter they did not fare so well; but they managed to get some of the ground grain from the mill for their meal-cakes, and Faustina made very good cheeses, and they lived even better than most of the poor folk in the country round about.

The village people had nothing good to say about Faustina. They were envious of her because she could live in a little home of her own, and had means enough, however small, to be independent of her neighbors. Some said she was vain, and felt

her quality, because many years ago a well-to-do
worker in stone from the city had come and married her. She was young and pretty then — they
called upon the good saints to witness that she had
once been pretty, with almond-shaped black eyes
and apple-red cheeks, though no one would suspect
it now, Santa Maria! And she had not been too
proud to dance and feast with them on her wed-
ding-day. But he had taken her off to the city to
live with him, and that had given her such notions
of grandeur that she could no longer mingle with
old friends at the village, but must have a hut all
to herself, though the good Saint Peter alone knew
how she ever scraped up enough to pay the rental
every year, and she must needs put on airs and
shun her old companions as if they had been a
pestilence, they said.

It was well enough to be proud and disdainful
of one's neighbors when one had one's own hut to
sleep in, and could dig one's own turnips and artichokes; but this not having any friends looked
very ill to the genial people of Galluzzo. A cat
and a slip of a boy were her only companions —
well, she might better have been a hermit, and have
done with it! and let the boy and the cat enjoy
themselves elsewhere.

There were those who thought Faustina must have committed some wicked sin, and that she was living alone in this solitary and mysterious way for a penance; others, who were not so sour-minded, said she had broken her heart when her husband and her own little boy had died, and that she could not bear to see others happy, with their children and loved ones around them; and that she had taken the boy, that he might work for her and support her when she grew old and disabled. However all this might be, Faustina minded them no more than the cat minded her, and she cared not a fig for their opinion. All that she asked was that they should leave her in peace, and not stop too long to pry into her garden on their way down the road, and not lure Raffaello with sweetmeats to talk about things he did not know.

One evening the three were seated round the little table in the kitchen, eating their supper. I say the three, for Minnetto was regarded as one of the family, and Faustina would not have sat down to a meal without him any more than without Raffaello. It was the early spring-time, and they had not yet lighted the candle. Faustina had walked to and from the city that day, as she did sometimes; and as it was a long distance off, she was weary

" The strange little family."

and cross when she returned. But she had brought home a little cake for which she had parted with some of her strawberries, and she was cutting it into exactly three pieces as she addressed Raffaello and the cat.

" Now what have you done all day, you two idle ones, while I have been blistering my feet to sell a few cents' worth of berries to buy you bread, and cake, too, cake, indeed! for a *bimbo*[1] who cannot earn a *centessimo;*[2] and a cat who does nothing but eat and sleep, and never cares where the next meal is to come from ? " As she spoke she flung a third of the cake into each plate, and without wait-ing a reply, turned suddenly upon Minnetto, who had fallen with both paws upon his piece and was gnawing at one corner of it with great relish : " You don't deserve a morsel, you lazy, yellow-eyed mon-ster ! I found a mouse in the grain-bag to-night. How long is it since you 've caught a mouse ? "

Minnetto went on munching at the brown cake and purring contentedly, winking his golden eyes, as much as to say, " Little do I care for the mice in the grain-bag. I 'm too fat to run after them, and too well-fed to want them ! "

Raffaello sat looking at his cake without tasting

[1] A little boy. [2] One fifth of a cent.

it. He never took Faustina's grumbling with the
same philosophy as Minnetto. He had listened to it
very, very often; there was scarcely a day that Faustina did not scold about something; but he could
not grow used to it and not care, like Minnetto, —
that was only the difference between being a boy
and being a cat. Her words, especially when they
were reproachful, always made him sad and sorry;
and he thought to-night how tired and worn she
seemed, and how hard she really worked to get the
little money they needed to live and pay the land-
lord, and he was wondering how he could help her,
and in what way he might earn a few *soldi* to give
her, for she said so often that he was of no use to
her.

"What are you gaping at?" said Faustina, sharply,
seeing that Raffaello was thinking. "Why don't you
eat your supper! *Ecco,*[1] have you been up to some
mischief, and has your conscience got into your
stomach, to make you sniff at a good brown cake
just fresh from the baker's?"

"Oh, no, Faustina," and he glanced at the cat for
a witness, "I have been a good *bimbo* all day. I
have fed the canary, and fetched some wood from
the road, and watered the artichokes, and picked

---

[1] A favorite exclamation of the Florentines.

more berries to send — to take into the city to-
morrow."

" To take into the city ! " repeated Faustina, in a
vexed tone. " It is easy to say 'take into the city '
when somebody else does the walking. It takes
feet to go to the city, good stout ones, too, and if
one is n't a mule, one cannot go every day to earn
a half-franc ! "

" I know, Faustina, I know it makes you very
tired; and I wish," added Raffaello, hesitating, " I
wish you would let me go instead, and sell the
flowers and the strawberries."

" You ! " cried Faustina, bringing her knife down
upon the table with such force, that even Minnetto
jumped. " You ! what would you do in the city but
get lost, and turn my hair white with searching for
you ! Florence is not like Galluzzo; it has a hundred streets, not one, and you would be a dead
bambino [1] before you had walked half the way, you
little pumpkin-head ! "

" I could go with Luigi. He has a cart and
donkey, and rides to town on all the *festa* days.
He would take me with him, and teach me the
streets, and bring me back in the evening; he has
said so."

[1] Baby.

" Humph! Luigi, Luigi," retorted Faustina, shrug-
ging her big shoulders, "he has a long tongue, has
Luigi! He has been here to-day?"

" Yes, he came to bring a piece of fowl; the *padrona* sent it for our dinner to-morrow."

Faustina's black eyes gleamed suspiciously. The
padrona was Luigi's mother, one of the few women
at the village who thought charitably and pitifully
of Faustina, and she would often send one of her
boys, on a Saturday, with some bit of her cookery,
a rib or two of sheep, or a half of a young rooster,
or some such dainty to make the Sunday more
cheerful for Faustina and the little boy. But Faustina was afraid of her kindness, and seldom touched
any of the gifts herself, dividing them between Raffaello and the cat, so fearful was she of establishing
friendly or intimate relations with any of her old
companions at Galluzzo.

" And he put the silly notion in your head, did
he?" resumed Faustina, after a long pause, during
which she seemed to have been thinking unpleasant
thoughts.

" I spoke to him first," said Raffaello, "and asked
him why he went so often to the city, and he told
me that he carried the milk and butter there for his
mother, who cannot go herself on account of the

bambino; and that now, when the flowers are coming out, he and his brothers would stop on their way
down the hill to gather a basketful of violets and
lilies, and take them to the *piazza*[1] to sell; and that
sometimes, they came home with their pockets full
of *soldi*, which they gave to their mother. And I
said I would like to go to the city and sell flowers,
and bring the money to you."

Raffaello's little face had grown quite flushed with
the ardor of his good intention, and his dark eyes
looked up earnestly and appealingly at the hard face
across the table.

" It is well enough for Luigi and his brothers to
go to the city, and come back with their pockets
full of *soldi*. They are big country lads, much older
than you, and brazen-faced young rascals who are
not ashamed to beg when they have nothing more
to sell. You are not a beggar, do you hear ! we will
starve first, but you shall not beg."

Here Faustina gave Minnetto a frightful tweak
of the ear, for no reason at all that Raffaello could
see, and Minnetto promptly repaid her with a revengeful spat of his paw, and went on with his
supper as indifferently as before.

Raffaello did not quite understand what Faustina

[1] Public square.

meant by these last words. He had often heard
her say, " It is only the lazy common folk who beg.
You do not belong to the common people, and you
shall never beg, while I live to prevent it." So he had
come to regard begging, in his little mind, as a very
wicked and unworthy thing, and would never have
thought of doing it if Faustina had not repeated this
so often. But he could see nothing wrong in his
wanting to serve Faustina as Luigi and Giulio
served their mother, and his little head was full of
the thought.

" If you will let me go with Luigi, Faustina, once
every week, before Sunday and on the *festas*, I will
bring home enough *soldi*, perhaps, to buy all we need;
and when I am as tall as Luigi, I will buy you a
little cart and mule, and then we can ride to the
city together, and you need never get tired any
more." He had left his place at the table, and was
standing quite close to Faustina's side, with a demure
look of entreaty that sat strangely upon his childish
face.

Faustina did not take any notice of him at all.
She went on eating her bread very fast, and taking
great gulps of milk, without saying a word for several
minutes.

" If they should lose him, Santa Maria! if they

should lose him!" she muttered, not addressing any one, "and he should fall into worse hands than mine, and I could never find him, or dare search for him! O Heaven! what a mad thought!" and she smoothed the wrinkles from her forehead with the coarse towel on her lap, and pushed Raffaello away from her, but not impatiently, and said aloud, "Go sit upon the door-steps and count the fireflies till bed time. I am not to be troubled now, my head is too weary. Go, you and Minnetto."

Raffaello obeyed, and the big cat immediately jumped down and followed him to the door, where they both sat on the old gray stone, Minnetto licking his chops assiduously, and curling his long tail around his feet, for a comfortable meditation; while little Raffaello pursued his own thoughts in the quiet of the soft spring evening, and the little river murmured its winding way down the pretty valley of the Ema.

CHAPTER II

FAUSTINA remained at the table long after the night had settled and the little hut was dark. Her head had fallen on her arms, which rested on the table, and she seemed to be asleep; but she was not.

She was only thinking, thinking so silently, so deeply, that Raffaello did not dare to disturb her when he came in. He closed the outer door very gently, gave Minnetto one or two love-pats, and slipped quietly into the little closet which was his sleeping-room.

Raffaello was a very little boy as yet, but his living with two such wise and tried philosophers as Faustina and Minnetto had made a very sage of him for his years. Yet he had no great cares on his mind,

no great troubles in his heart, no fearful dread of
the future, and no sad memories of the past. He
was not unhappy; for although Faustina spoke
gruffly, and was not over gentle with him, she never
maltreated him, or willingly made him suffer. Her
only thought seemed to be that he should want
nothing, and she toiled for him early and late, and
spared herself no hardship, that he might have
enough to eat and wear, and that he might not look
like the ragged little beggars of the city and village
streets. Raffaello did not have that same fondness
for her which he might have had for a tender
mother who would have fondled him, and loved
him, and spoken gentle words to him, and taught
his young heart to open freely; but he was at-
tached to her, as children are to those who protect
them, and cared for her as well as he knew how to
care for any one. And to-night he was full of the
idea of doing something for her, of helping her to
earn their livelihood, and saving her tired feet by
using his young ones in their stead, for he knew that
Faustina was very poor. " Perhaps," he thought,
as he lay upon his straw mattress in the dark, " if I
could sell flowers in the big city, and earn enough
soldi to buy the grain every week, it would make
Faustina happy, and she would not be cross any

more." And when he fell asleep, his thoughts suffered no interruptions, for he dreamed that he and
Luigi were already started for Florence, and that on
their way, they came upon a vast field of daisies,
and when they stooped to gather the flowers, they
saw that in the heart of each blossom there was a
small round coin of gold, like the one Faustina
kept locked in the tin box beside her bed, only that
hers had a hole, with a chain through it. And he
dreamed that they filled their baskets to the top
with the bright pieces and brought them home, and
when Faustina saw them, she fell on her knees and
kissed his hands, and cried, " O Raffaello mio ! [1]
you are rich, you are great, and they will take you
from me ! "

And this was only his dream. But what was
really true, was that far into the night, when Raffaello
was sleeping soundly, and the battered Madonna at
his bed-head seemed to be smiling a watch over
him, and Minnetto was curled up into a dark bundle beside the ashes, snoozing with one eye open, as
was his habit, Faustina had crept to Raffaello's
couch, and was kneeling beside it, and kissing his
hand indeed, and saying in a low voice, " He wants
to work for me, *Dio mio !* for me ! the poor *bam-*

[1] My Raffaello.

bino, and so little, so little ! O Raffaello mio, you are rich, rich, and they will find you out and take you from me ! "

She kneeled there for a long time, praying to the Madonna above, and looking at the face of the sleeping child, so peaceful and unconscious ; and no one saw or heard, not even the cat, who was accustomed to Faustina's nightly tread about the rooms, for everything was sleeping except the bright star that twinkled through the casement, and shed its mysterious light on the sleeping child and the praying woman. If any one could have looked in besides the star, he would have seen that Faustina's face was not so hard now, and that she hung over the little boy as tenderly as if she had been his own mother, and that her black eyes were wet, and her lip trembled. Faustina had her own reasons for not teaching Raffaello to love her too well ; but secretly she cherished him, and no one knew how much but the star, who was too far away to tell of what it saw, sometimes, in the night.

The next morning was Sunday, and Faustina was up with the sun to attend the early mass at the church of San Gaggio, which is about half-way down on the road to the city of Florence. Raffaello heard the jingling of her beads, as she went out and closed the door, and immediately he was on his feet, and dressing himself, taking up his little project just where he had left it the night before. He reckoned that Faustina must walk over a mile before she reached San Gaggio; that would take nearly a half-hour, although she took long steps like a man, and never stopped to chat with neighbors, or loitered on her way. Then the mass would take another half hour, and she could scarcely get back before the bells of La Certosa di Val[1] had sounded the seventh hour. This would give him plenty of time to run down into the valley and gather a basketful of red and yellow tulips and white crocuses that grew wild along the borders of the brooklet Ema. He took a little osier-basket which hung in the kitchen, the one Faustina used to carry her strawberries when she went to the market-place, and laid some fresh mulberry leaves at the bottom of it, that his' flowers might have a moist, green bed to lie on. Then he set out quietly, not wishing to rouse Minnetto, who was an inquisitive old pussy, and who would have to be coaxed very hard to remain behind if he suspected any frolic in the air. Minnetto had not moved an

---

[1] An old monastery situated just above the village of Galluzzo.

eye-winker all through Faustina's preparations for church, but when he spied Raffaello's heels disappearing behind the lattice, he gave a sudden bound towards the door, and mewed reproachfully at the disappearing figure of his little master. He made a gingerly attempt to follow, but Raffaello was running very fast, and the grass was heavily covered with dew; and Minnetto detested the wet, so he thought better of it, and turned back to his corner near the hearth, where he sat licking his paws and wagging his tail in much discontent.

The morning was such a bright one, the early sun was so warm, and the breeze was so cool, and the young grass-blades sparkled so with their beads of fresh dew, and the air was so sweet with the scent of the olive blossoms, that Raffaello's heart was very light, and he wondered why it was that he felt so much happier than he had ever felt before. He was too little to know that it was the hope of helping Faustina more than the beautiful spring morning, and the sweet air, and the refreshing dew, that made his feet swift and his heart glad. He did not know yet that the one thing in this world that brings us the truest happiness and the sweetest reward is helping some fellow-creature whom Heaven has placed in our way, however young our

hands, however small our means. He was too
much a child to understand this, for he was not
much more than six years old, and so little, so little,
as Faustina had said, that he seemed always like a
baby. But I think that somewhere in his childish
nature the seeds of that great truth were firmly
rooted.

It did not take him long to fill his basket with
fresh flowers, and return to the hut, where he soon
made his peace with Minnetto for having slipped
away from him, by making a cheery blaze with some
fagots, and putting the pot of milk on to boil.
With these promising preparations, Minnetto became quite forgiving, and the two were sitting close
together on the floor, watching the steaming breakfast when Faustina returned.

She was in a better mood than she had been on
the previous evening. She was always in a better
mood when she came home from the mass; for I
think the solemn quiet of the old church, and the
soothing tones of the chanting monks, and the
beautiful faces of the saints and the Madonnas that
looked down at her from the walls and windows,
comforted her, and gave her strength to pass
another solitary and friendless week.

They had just finished their breakfast, and Raf-

"It was Luigi and his brothers."

faëllo was wondering how he would best renew his
cherished subject with Faustina, for he felt sure that
she would not hold out long when she saw how much
in earnest he was, and when he showed her the
pretty flowers all ready to go to the market-place,
which she had pretended not to notice when she
entered; when suddenly there came a mighty hal-
looing and shouting from out upon the road, as if all
the children in the village of Galluzzo had been let
loose for a holiday. Raffaello and Faustina ran to
the door, to see what it was all about. It was
Luigi and his brothers, a *troupe* of noisy, apple-faced
boys, who were thus disturbing the peace of the
quiet Sunday morning. They were all crowded
into the little market-cart, which was drawn by that
most stubborn, most obstinate member of the
family of Italian donkeys, Pierrota. All the children were standing up in the cart, except those
who were tumbling out of it, and some were pulling
vigorously at the reins as a hint to Pierrota to stop,
which she could not, under any consideration, think
of doing, she being by nature more disobliging and
more contrary-minded than any other donkey;
while the others were shouting to Raffaello to join
them, for they were on their way to the city.

  " Oh, let me go with them, Faustina," cried little

Raffaello, looking up at her and clutching her dress excitedly; " do, please, let me go, and I will be very good and not lose myself ! and see, I have the flowers all ready."

Faustina's hard face was very white, and her eyes had a frightened look in them. She did not give him a sharp no, as she did sometimes when he asked for anything she did not approve. She had not said no at any time about this, and he felt emboldened to plead yet a little more.

" I will not wander from the market-square, and when I have sold my flowers, I will sit down and wait till Luigi comes to bring me back."

All the while Luigi and his brothers kept up a constant invitation: " Come, come, *piccino*, come, there is still room for you and your basket. *Hiu !* Diavolino ! " This last was addressed to the donkey, who was still pursuing her course, slowly but resolutely.

" Hold your tongues, you shouting young rascals ! " cried Luigi, above the rest. " Let the *bimbo* come with us, Monna Faustina. I 'll take good care of him, and bring him back safe. I 'll look after the *piccino !* "

Luigi, being the eldest of the lads, made a great matter of his importance, and his ability to take care of them all, being the biggest and tallest of the lot. He was a good, hearty, wholesome boy of twelve or thereabouts, and his brothers were very much like him, with just that difference in their height that made them look like a nicely graded pair of stairs when they stood in a row. They always called Raffaello *piccino*, " the little one," because he was so small beside even the youngest of them, and his face was so fine and delicate beside their ruddy ones.

Faustina had stepped back into the room, and presently returned with the basket of flowers, and a paper bundle which she handed to Raffaello.

" There is the fowl and the bread for your dinner," she said; " take it along, you will get no other. And you, Luigi," and she raised her voice for the benefit of the lads on the road, " see that you bring him back whole, and that you keep out of mischief, every one of you, or I 'll — "

But by this time, the donkey had achieved such a goodly distance from the hut, in spite of the jerking at her bridle, that Luigi did not hear her threat. Little Raffaello was so delighted with Faustina's sudden decision, that he immediately hugged the cat, who yawned with dignified surprise; and then he took up his basket, said good-bye to Faustina, and ran as fast as he could after the little cart.

Faustina and Minnetto stood watching him from the door of the stone hut: she with the softer look in her large black eyes and her bony fingers clasped tightly together, as she repeated, " Holy Madonna! look to him. Perhaps I am a fool for letting him go out of my sight; but something tells me that only good can come of it for him, and I have kept him to myself alone long enough, and my conscience is sore with pricking."

As for Signor Minnetto, he was not following quite the same line of thought as that of his mistress. His pride was touched at having been twice deserted by his little friend that morning, — by Raffaello, who so rarely went anywhere without him, — and he presently turned away from the scene with a superior and indifferent air, as one who should say, " What this stupid business is all about, I am sure I don't know, and be it far from me to care!"

I T was some time before Raffaello was safely landed in the cart, for Pierrota, the donkey, though a small creature, had a mighty will, and all the pulling and jerking at her iron jaw made no more impression on her than if she had been a wooden donkey going by machinery. The lads managed to lift Raffaello in, while the cart was still moving slowly, for Pierrota had ideas of her own about speed; and when the feat was accomplished, after much screaming and laughing, Luigi cracked his willow switch in a business-like manner, and shouted, " Now, then, you little beast, get along ! "

But this was the last of the gentle Pierrota's intentions. As soon as the occasion for stopping was past, she immediately stood stock-still, and could no more be persuaded to budge than if her four hoofs had been stout grip-hooks clinched in the earth under her. To " get along " when she was

bidden to do so, was as much against her principles as it was to stop by request, and Pierrota
was nothing if not a donkey of principles. They
coaxed and threatened, they prodded and switched,
they got out and pushed the cart on to her, they
pulled at her bridle with all their might; but it was
of no use. She only stiffened her long ears, and
allowed her body to sway forward a trifle; but her
legs were as firm as rocks. It was a full quarter of
an hour after Luigi and his companions had sur-
rendered to her superior strength, and were waiting,
panting and exhausted with their exertions, when
Pierrota made up her cast-iron mind to pursue her
course down the beautiful road leading to the Porta
Romana.[1]

It was Raffaello's first ride to the city, and he was
much interested in the other country folk who were
also going to Florence, some in festive Sunday attire,
with bright colored skirts and kerchiefs, and white
aprons, carrying their provisions to the market-place,
and doubtless intending to remain after their morning's trade for the mass at the big Duomo,[2] where
they would hear the fine preaching and the good
music. Luigi and his brothers seemed to know

---

[1] Roman gate, one of the many gates of Florence.
[2] The cathedral.

everybody on the road, and had a jovial good-morn-
ing for each as they met; and little Raffaello's
admiration for his friends grew at every mile-stone.
He would soon be a tall stout lad, like Luigi, he
thought, and then he could drive a cart himself, and
take Faustina and Minnetto with him, since he had
no young brothers like Luigi, and they would go to
the *festas* he had heard so much about, and there
would always be *quattrini*[1] enough to buy what
Faustina wanted, and she would never be cross to him
and the cat.   Oh, it was a happy, happy morning for
Raffaellino, but he could not talk of his happiness to
his little comrades; he could only sit and think
about it quietly, while they laughed and joked
among themselves, and appealed to him every now
and then with " Eh, *piccino ?* "

When they reached the great city gate, and had
turned into the Via Romana,[2] towards the Ponte
Vecchio,[3] Raffaello began to notice the great change
between the bright, green, sunlit country, and the
gray stone city, with its high buildings and narrow
streets, and its crowds of people hurrying to and
from the churches, whose near and distant bells
were clanging a weird and tuneless harmony.

[1] The smallest Italian coin.   [2] Roman Street.
[3] The Old Bridge.

"We shall not go to the *mercato*," said Luigi, "it is too late. That stubborn beast of a Pierrota has made us lose too much time with her meditations on the way;" for they had had one or two more contests with the donkey before reaching the city.

The Via Romana.

"We will go to the Piazza del Duomo with our flowers, for the people will soon be coming to the High Mass."

No one made any objections; no one ever made any objections to Luigi's views, except, perhaps, Pierrota sometimes. But even she suddenly put

on her good behavior when she entered the city,
and very soon they were crossing the Ponte Vecchio, and Raffaello could see between the low arches
of the covered bridge the beautiful, silvery Arno
flowing smoothly through the heart of the old city,
and the fair slopes of Bello Sguardo and Mount
Oliveto rising on its south bank; while on the
north, the great tower of the old palace, and
the dark mass of Santa Croce,[1] and the dome of the
cathedral towered above the whole city. Truly,
Florence was a very wonderful place. He had
never dreamed of anything like it, and the little village of Galluzzo, which was the only place he remembered having ever visited with Faustina, was
like an ant-hill beside this.

When they came to the square in front of the
cathedral, the place was already filled with people,
and many other young flower-vendors, who had
made an earlier start, were running after the ladies,
holding up their fresh nosegays, singing lustily:
" All for two cents ! Only two cents ! "

Luigi lost no time in tumbling out of the cart,
and assisted Raffaello to do likewise, and then he
led the donkey around into one of the side streets,
and fastened a long feed-bag about Pierrota's neck,

---

[1] One of the largest churches in the city.

into which her nose suddenly disappeared, that she might entertain herself with a little refreshment until their return. The other lads had fled in various directions as soon as they were on their feet, for in their eagerness to join in the excitement of the trade, they quite forgot that Raffaello was a timid little stranger in the big city. When Luigi re-appeared from around the corner, he found the little boy standing alone in the shadow of the tall bell-tower, his basket of tulips on his arm, and looking about him in a helpless way.

" Ha, those young rabbits ! " Luigi cried, " they have all skipped off and left you, *piccino*. Well, come with me; I will find you a good place to sit, where you can see the people pass and offer them your flowers, and where I can find you when I come back. For you must not run about, lest you should get into trouble. Faustina would call down maledictions on my head, and never let you come again."

Raffaello promised not to stir from the place where Luigi led him, and they crossed the square to the Bigallo, which is a small open porch in the Cathedral Square, where, in olden times, the poor children of the city were brought to receive charities. There he sat upon the steps, and was quite hidden by the crowd. " Now stay right here on the *piazza*, and

" There he sat, upon the steps."

sell all your flowers by the time I come again, that's a good *bimbo!* And let's see which one of us can show the most *soldi!*" and Luigi sallied off with his own stock-in-trade to the neighboring streets and haunts he knew so well.

But this was hardly as encouraging a proposal as it sounded, for poor Raffaello was so very inexperienced in the business, and felt so timid when he found himself all alone in this strange place, with so many new faces going by him all the time, that he had not the courage to call out, " Belle fiori ! " like the other lads; and even if he had, I doubt whether his childish voice could have been heard or his tiny figure noticed by that gay multitude of Sunday strollers. The little fellow had not the least notion of how he should go about the selling of his flowers. The thought that he must run after people boldly and thrust a handful of blossoms in their faces, and shout, " Two cents! " in their ears, had never entered his small head. So he sat quietly gazing at the lovely white church opposite and the fair, slender bell-tower, and at all the people going in at the doors of the Duomo, till he began to wish that he, too, might cross the *piazza* and look in at its portals to see the glorious faces of the Holy Madonna and angels, which Luigi said he had once seen there. He could hear the sound of voices chanting every time the doors opened to let the worshippers pass in and out, and it seemed to him as if he must be very near Paradise, and that the beautiful entrance to the cathedral must be the gate that led thither. But every one went by without looking at him, or buying any of his flowers; and by and by he began to be a little discouraged, and after a long while, very lonely.

It must have been nearly two hours that he sat there as still as a little mouse, wondering when Luigi and his brothers would return, when he was suddenly seized with a desire to walk to the edge of the street and get a glimpse of Pierrota, who was placidly and contentedly munching the contents of her bag in the narrow street around the corner. Pierrota was only a donkey, to be sure; but it would be comforting to see some familiar creature just now, and her loud and frequent braying had served to remind Raffaello, from time to time, that he had a friend near at hand. He stepped to the very edge of the walk, and was leaning as far as he could to look down into the street at Pierrota, when a carriage dashed by so near, and with such speed, that the little boy was startled, and dropped his basket in the road, and all his pretty flowers were scattered and crushed by the big dusty wheels.

"*Capperi!*" exclaimed a tremendously deep voice from the box. "Will the plagued youngsters never learn to get out of the way! Perdition take you for stopping my horse when I'm in such a hurry! *Ecco!* a little more, and you would have gone under with your flowers — a pestilence on them! and I should have had to pay the magistrate for your broken neck!"

Raffaello was so frightened that he began to cry, not so much at what the big, burly, red-faced man said, for he really seemed to be smiling even while he scolded lustily, as at the sudden turn he had received, and at the sight of all his pretty flowers lying dead in the road.

"Look at him! the *bambino* is crying, now," said the burly man, reining in his horse and jumping from his coach. "There, there, don't fret yourself any more. I'll forgive you for coming in my way, and will not give you any penance this time; but mind you don't do it again, else I will call on all the little imps to roast your ears," and he patted Raffaello kindly on the shoulder, in spite of his terrible threat.

Raffaello had not thought of the coachman's forgiveness as a means of consolation for the loss of his posies. He stooped to pick up the injured blossoms, drawing his little sleeve across his eyes.

"What, blubbering still! What more do you want, you silly young rabbit?"

"Oh, my flowers, my flowers!" sobbed Raffaello.

"Is that all? Ho, ho, ho!" roared the big *cocchiere*,[1] "Why, the fields are full of them, and there are plenty more where those came from. Besides, of what good are your silly flowers? —you can't make salad of them, or boil them down for spinach."

"I was going to sell them, and take the money to Faustina," explained Raffaello, as he placed each one back in the basket.

"And will Monna Faustina beat you, if you don't bring home the *quattrini ?* "

"Oh, no, signor! Faustina does not beat me, nor even Minnetto."

"And who is Minnetto?" inquired the man.

"Minnetto is our cat."

"Then, Faustina is a good woman, and does not ill-use you?" demanded the red-faced *cocchiere*, quite overlooking the fact that he was in such a hurry, in his interest to learn more about the little fellow.

"Faustina is very good to me," said Raffaello; and he likewise lost sight of his trouble for a moment, as he glanced up with wonder, ever so high, into the face of the old cabman who was so big and good-

---

[1] Cabman.

natured, and had such a purplish hue to his com-
plexion, and such a wonderful nose, and who had so
many brass buttons to his coat, and wore such an
enormous glazed hat over one ear, that Raffaello
believed he must be some grand personage, and
insisted on calling him signor. The little boy had
never seen any one so remarkable before, and he
fancied he must be very rich to sit a-top such a
splendid coach and drive a horse, not a simple coun-
try-donkey, like Pierrota.

"*Altro!* Then you ought not to care a fig about
the flowers, since Faustina will not beat you!" and
he snapped his fat fingers in the air, with a conclu-
sive nod.

"But I wanted very much to sell them, so as to
give Faustina the money. We are poor, and she
has to work hard. Now, no one will buy them,"
said Raffaello, his face falling again at the recollec-
tion of his misfortune.

"*Che, che!* then you are a good *bimbo!*" said
the coachman, as if the discovery of a good boy
were quite a new thing to him. Then, plunging
violently into his waistcoat pocket, he added, "By
San Giovanni! since you are a good *bimbo*, and a
pretty *bimbo* into the bargain," and he tilted Raffaello's face far back, the better to look in it, — "yes

a pretty *bimbo!* I'll give you a few cents for your flowers, such as they are. I will take them to the *madre.*[1] She is very old, is the *madre,* and she can neither see nor hear nor smell. She'll never mind the dust and the broken stems. She'll feel them with her hands, and think herself back in the country instead of an old garret. But you must not charge me for the dust. What will you take for them, dust and all?"

"Oh, I don't know, signor, whatever you like!"

"That's a fine way of trading, San Pietro! Whatever I like! It might be one *quattrino,* if I were a poor beggar of a coachman, or a hundred francs, if I were the Duke of Vallambrosa!"

Raffaello did not understand this bit of ratio and proportion. He looked at the big cabman with astonishment in his eyes, and a flush of expectation on his round baby face.

"Now what do you say to two cents, ten bright *centissimi?*" he said, bargaining wholly with himself, not with Raffaello. "No? not two? Three, then, three cents!"

"Get along with you! three cents indeed! that would not pay for the nails in the shoes a *bimbo* wears to walk in from the country. A *lira!*"[2]

---

[1] Mother.

[2] The standard of Italian money, — worth twenty cents.

"A *lira!* forty apoplexies on you! What do
you think I am made of? Do you think I get the
rentals of the Villa Barborello!"

"Eighty *centissimi,* then."

"No more eighty : you may keep your tulips, and
put them in your soup-pot to flavor your Sunday
dinner. I'll give you fifty for them, not a *quattrino*
more. Fifty, is it?"

"That's too little; but let it be fifty, though
that's a bad bargain for me, a very bad bargain."

After concluding this little dialogue with himself,
— it was only a habit he had of bargaining whenever he made any sort of purchase, — he drew a
battered leathern purse from his pocket, took out
a new silver piece, fifty *centissmi,* worth just ten
cents, and handed it to Raffaello with a smile of
immense satisfaction.

"There's a fortune for you, my little man! May
you never meet with worse luck!"

"Oh, thank you! thank you so much, *signor!*"
cried Raffaello, joyfully, eying the bright coin.
"Faustina will be so glad!"

"There, there," returned the coachman, waving
him off, "no thanks are needed for a good bargain,
on either side. I must be off; I'm in a tremendous hurry, I tell you!"

He opened the door of his cab, and flung Raffaello's flowers on the seat. "Now, see that you don't get in the way of my wheels again," he added, slamming the coach-door; "but if you do, remember that my name is Camillo, and my number is twenty-one, and that I live behind the Badia.[1] What's your name?"

"My name is Raffaello."

Camillo nodded as if the name were satisfactory.

"Well! Raffaello is a good name for a *bimbo* with a pretty face." With which he mounted his coach once more, flourished his whip several times over his head, and, with a broad smile for Raffaello, drove away.

By this time the crowd was beginning again, for the people were coming out of the cathedral, and the mass was over; so Raffaello slipped back to his little corner on the steps of the Bigallo, holding his empty basket in one hand, and clutching his precious silver piece in the other. It was not long before Luigi and his brothers returned and found the little boy just where they had left him.

"San Pietro!" exclaimed Luigi, "the *piccino's* basket is empty! Did you sell them all, Raffaellino?"

"Yes, a grand *signor* in a carriage took them all;

[1] The Badia is one of the oldest churches in Florence.

he bought them for his old mother." And he related as correctly as his distorted imagination would allow, all that had taken place between him and Camillo.

" And how much did he give you ? " was the eager question.

Raffaello spread out his palm and showed the silver piece with great pride.

" Santa Maria, what good fortune! You 're a lucky one, *piccino*," the lads all shouted in a chorus; and indeed, he had been much luckier than they. For although each one had sold his little stock, and was jingling his fifteen, twenty, or thirty *centissimi* in his pocket as he danced his pleasure, not one of them had earned as much as fifty, not even Luigi.

They all tumbled into the cart once more; and as Pierrota was always pleased with the prospect of turning her nose homeward, everything went as merry as a marriage-bell, and they were very soon out of the city, and again upon the open country road, eating their dinners as they went, and feeling as happy as country lads always do the world over.

But the happiest of them all, I think, was little Raffaello; for the morning had, in truth, brought him much good-fortune, — more than he really knew of at the time, for he had made his first acquaintance with the beautiful city of Florence, and earned a shining piece of silver for Faustina, and gained, what is still more precious, a good friend.

CHAPTER FOURTH

OU may imagine with what a glad heart Faustina saw the little cart coming up the brow of the hill, as she stood at the door of her stone hut, late that afternoon. She had not done much else than come to the door and watch, though she knew they could scarcely get back till long after the church hour; for poor Pierrota found it a slow and difficult task to draw a cartful of stout lads up the steep road. Whatever indiscretion or frivolity she might have indulged in on her way down, she never showed any but a meek and docile spirit on her way up the hill, as if from each trip she returned a sadder but a wiser donkey.

It was four o'clock when Pierrota stopped in front of Faustina's dwelling. Raffaello, after saying good-

bye to Luigi and his brothers, ran to Faustina, eager
to relate all that had happened, and to show her the
fruit of his success. She was more eager, if possible, to hear it all, than he was to tell it; and she
sat and looked intently at his animated little face,
his large liquid eyes, and the bright color that rose
to his cheeks as he spoke. She had never seen him
so excited, and he seemed to have grown and
changed in that one day of absence, the first he
had ever spent away from her since he had been in
her keeping. When he had finished his adventures,
Faustina kissed him on the forehead, and Raffaello
was happy, for she rarely did this unless she had
some great reason for being pleased with him.

"And you are glad that I went, now, Faustina,
are you not?" he asked.

"Glad that you got into no worse mischief?
yes, I am glad," she said, in her same old tones.

"And you will let me go again?"

"Yes, yes, but not too often; it is not well for
country lads to see too much of the city."

After that, Faustina was silent, and remained so
all the rest of that day. She seemed to be thinking, thinking very gloomily about something, and
she went about the house in an absent-minded sort
of way, sweeping up the cat with the crumbs with-

out knowing it, and watering the canary instead
of the artichokes. Their hut, of only two rooms, —
the one where Faustina slept and said her prayers,
the other where they cooked and ate and worked by
the fire on long winter evenings, together with the
little closet which was Raffaello's, — had always
seemed like a very large and roomy house; and so it
was, in comparison with the way in which most poor
families lived yonder at Galluzzo, where every one
found fault with her for living in such luxury!
While in truth, she had just enough to live misera-
bly, which to those who have nothing, seems a great
deal. But to-night the little house seemed terribly
poor and bare to Faustina, in spite of the small fortune Raffaello had brought her. The air of the
room seemed to choke her, the ceiling seemed to be
pressing down upon her, and she could not sit
quietly beside the window and tell her beads, as was
her custom on Sunday evenings. She walked
about the place restlessly, and at length went out
into the small garden that she might breathe more
freely and give more room to her thoughts.

What is she thinking of as she sits on the little
stone bench underneath the tall cypress, and the
darkening twilight is falling about her? Her lips
are set very tight, and her black eyes are looking

far, far away, farther than where the brooklet Ema
turns its course, farther than where the old *certosa*
crowns the hill of Montaguto. She is looking into
the twenty years that have passed since she was a
light-hearted village maid, with no more care or
thought of sorrow than the joyous nightingale that
wakened her in the morning. She recalls the time
when a good man had come and made her his wife,
and taken her with him to live in beautiful Florence.
It was just at this time, in the spring, twenty years
ago, after the glorious Easter, that he had taught her
to be happy, as people are but once in their lives, be
they lofty or lowly, be they rich or poor, famous or
obscure. What difference does it make? happiness
is happiness, no matter where it falls. But above
all she remembers the little stranger, the sweet
bambino that came to make the new year glad for
them. She smiles as she thinks of that time, for
the memory of it cannot be taken from her, although
sorrow came soon after. Before the return of
another spring, she had lost them both, the good
husband and the sweet babe, and she was mad with
grief. Ah, that was when the trouble all began, and
the wicked, bitter feeling took root in her heart!

They were repairing one of the bridges across the
Arno, the Ponte Rubaconte, the one leading to the

" What is she thinking of ? "

Piazza Santa Croce; she had good cause to remember it, and never to tread upon its accursed stones.
Her husband was at work there, and a huge slab
slipped and fell while they were raising it, and
crushed his life out of him. Then, the *bambino*
took a fever, from her taking him so much to the
cold, damp churches, where she went to say masses
for the soul of her poor husband, and the little
thing died too; and she was left alone and wretched,
worse off than if she had never known any joy,
and she could not make her peace with God, who
had brought her to such misery.

It is a pitiful thing to see people grow hard and
rebellious under the misfortunes which Providence
sees fit to send them, forgetting that these come
upon us only for a good purpose, — to chasten and
strengthen us, to test our faith perhaps, and teach
us to look to the world above if we would have the
knowledge of true joy.

Faustina lived in a fearful state of mind for twelve
years after the loss of her dear ones. She saw no
one; she would listen to no comfort or reason; she
did not even pray; she bound her heart with steel
that she might never learn to care for any thing or
creature again.

One day at dusk, — it was on a Thursday, when

the beautiful Gardens of Boboli are open to the
people until sun-down, and thousands flock thither
from their great stone prisons, to enjoy the new
spring air and verdure, — Faustina was walking
down the green maze of trees that leads to the
outer wall of the Porta Romana. It was her last
day in Florence, and she was going to the country
to live. She had secured the little hut for a small
rent, and it was just far enough from the village of
Galluzzo to enable her to lead the secluded and
lonely life she had chosen, and to keep away from
the too frequent sight of others' happiness. She
had worked hard, those twelve years, to save a little
money, and she could still braid straw for the
factories, and do her own gardening, and thus live
without mingling much with a world she hated.
Florence was sickening to her; there was no longer
any beauty or good in it; she had been so wretched
there that she longed to turn her back upon it.
To do this the sooner, she had passed through the
great gate of the Pitti Palace, and turned into one
of those long shady avenues of the Gardens which
stretch southward for nearly a mile, and finally open
upon the country road which she should take to
reach her new home. She had avoided the places
in the Gardens where the fountains play, and where

the crowds gather, — the crowds of gay young
women with their lovers and husbands, of mothers
with their children and grandchildren, and such a
multitude of nurse-maids in their bright dresses and
long-ribboned caps, carrying little ones in their arms,
that one would think a poor little *bimbo* like the
one Faustina had lost, would scarcely have been
missed. Oh, but that one little child left a greater
void in Faustina's heart than if all the other children of Florence had been taken away.

She stopped once to rest, just a few paces before
she reached the south gate. The sun was very low,
and the darkness had already entered the shady
walk from which she was emerging. It was very
quiet and solemn. She could no longer hear the
murmur of distant voices, as the crowd was moving
towards the principal entrance. She only heard the
faint tolling of the guard's bell, a warning that the
gates were about to close.

As she rose to go, a sound fell upon her ear. It
was a strange crackling sound, like the unsteady
pattering of small feet upon the gravel walk. As
it came nearer she heard a little cooing and gurgling
as of a contented young pigeon, and soon from a
narrow path intersecting the long avenue, there
appeared a wee, tottering figure looking about in

fearless surprise, evidently much delighted with each new discovery he had made in his lonely ramblings through that deserted part of the garden. The child uttered a little cry when he saw Faustina's tall dark figure, and ran towards her.

" Ma — ma!" cried the little thing, clutching her dress, and making inarticulate sounds to show that he was tired of his freedom, and wished to be taken care of.

With a sudden impulse, Faustina caught the child in her arms, and held it close. There was not another creature near. The little one had doubtless strayed from its nurse, and lost itself in the labyrinth of narrow paths. Faustina listened; but all was still as night, save for the baby's sleepy wail of " Ma — ma!" as its little head fell exhausted on her shoulder.

She stood only a moment irresolute. Then she hastily took from the bundle which she carried, containing her few possessions, an old shawl, which she wrapped about the child, and passed out of the gate upon the road without being seen of any one. She walked very fast, and her heart beat loud, and her cheeks grew hot, as she felt the little creature nestling to her bosom. She could not think of anything clearly, or realize what had happened until she had gone nearly half the way; but she kept repeating to herself, in a low husky voice: " I have not stolen it! I have not stolen it! It came to me. I will not give it up. Shall not others suffer as I have been made to suffer! Let them look, and search, and despair as I have done, they will never find

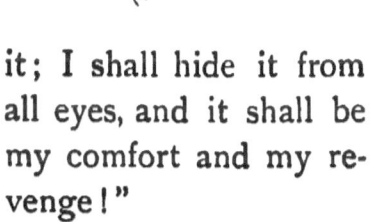

it; I shall hide it from all eyes, and it shall be my comfort and my revenge!"

With these bitter thoughts within her, Faustina journeyed on and on up the steep hill-road, never minding the descending night and the loneliness of the way, only clinging to the sleeping child more fiercely whenever she heard a sound, — a voice in the distance, or the far-off tinkle of a belated bullock returning homeward, or the rumbling of wheels over a bridge, or even the murmur of a vagrant streamlet scurrying over rocks. She feared lest any of them should be a pursuer who might overtake her before she had safely hidden her treasure, and she quickened her step, never stopping to listen until she had reached her journey's end.

The little hut was dark, and chill, and bare when she entered it ; but she minded not. It was a goodly distance from the village, and Galluzzo itself was such an out-of-the-way, forlorn, ignorant hamlet that it was the last place in the world where one would ever think of going to find anything or anybody. The village folk knew nothing of what took place at Florence. The tall figures on the Ponte San Trinita might have tumbled over into the Arno, and the people of Galluzzo would have been none the wiser ; for they took little interest in the things that did not concern them, and they were too simple and honest to be, themselves, suspicious of any mischief. So Faustina felt herself safe here, safer than she would have been anywhere else. She would shut herself away from everybody, that she might never hear of the search for the child; for a desperate search there would be, as indeed there was for days and nights, and weeks and months, in all the cities of Tuscany and Italy, everywhere but in the miserable village of Galluzzo.

She lighted the candle, and made a bit of fire with some small sticks which she had gathered before entering, and sat down in front of it to look at the small figure in her arms. It was a lovely babe, with rich dark curls, and large eyes whose closed lids were fringed with long beautiful lashes that swept his milk-white cheek. His little features were fine and delicate; and the smile that played upon the sleeping face made him look so like an angel, that she called him Raffaello. His clothes were made of rich, pure linen, beautifully hand-worked; and around his neck there hung, from a fine gold chain, a golden medal with the face of the Virgin upon it. Faustina quickly took off these things, and substituted for them some plainer and more humble garments that had belonged to her own babe. Then she took the pretty clothes, the fine silk hood, lace and all, and flung them into the fire, and watched the flames they made, till there was nothing left of them but a black fluttering heap. The medal she would not burn, for it was a sacred thing, and had been blessed by the priest; but she locked it safely away, in her little treasure-box, and sat the remainder of the night with the little one in her lap.

This was how it happened that Raffaello came to be a member of this strange little family. Everything had turned out as Faustina had hoped: no one came near for months; no one knew about the little boy she had with her, until several years after all this had taken place, and her fears and anxieties had worn away, little by little. She had only recently taken to going into the city; and now, once in a great while, she went with Raffaello to the village. But she made no explanations concerning him; and the people there had made their own conjectures. She had grown to care very much for the little boy, and could not have borne to part with him; though she never showed this by her manner, which was hard and sullen, lest he should grow to love her too well. But she was beginning to feel a little conscience-stricken for the great change she had been the means of bringing into his fortunes. As she often said, he was not of the common people, and she had tried to shield him, as much as she could, from terrible want and suffering; and now she had used up all her little store of money, and something must be

done to pay the *padrone*, or else they would be
turned out of the hut. That was why she had,
after much fearful thought, consented to let him
go to Florence that morning; and the event had
brought back to her all these painful remembrances,
and re-awakened all her fears, that for a time, at
least, seemed to have been sleeping.

This is what Faustina was thinking of as she
sat on the little stone bench underneath the tall
cypress, and the darkening night fell about her!

CHAPTER V

THERE is no lovelier country in all of lovely Italy than the fair plains of Tuscany. Tuscany, with its wealth of spring and summer flowers, and radiant verdure, its ancient trees, its grassy hill-slopes mantled with the tender green of the olive and the rosy flush of the blossoming almond, its rich vineyards and luxuriant fields where the red poppies and the yellow daffodils nod to one another from between the furrows, its shy wood-violets, and pure white stars-of-Bethlehem and sweet-scented gilliflowers lifting their bright faces to you wherever you tread; and the glorious warmth of its sunbeams, and the delicious coolness of its breezes, and the depth of blue in its skies, — surely it is no wonder that its people are the gay, light-hearted, smiling, songful nation that they are! And I

think there are no happier children in the world
than the Tuscan boys and girls, who live simple
lives, and enjoy simple pleasures, and who grow up
to manhood and womanhood surrounded by the
sweetest and purest joys that Nature can afford.

Raffaello, being a child of Tuscany, and therefore heir to all the gifts and blessings of that
smiling country, should have been happy indeed,
as happy as any of his little comrades yonder at
Galluzzo, especially now that a way was open to him
which promised to make him useful to Faustina.
He should have been happy, I say, save for the
vague consciousness he had that a mystery hung
over his lonely childhood. There was something
about the hut, about Faustina, even about the cat,
sometimes, that made him feel he did not hold the
same place there that other children held in their
homes. No one ever laughed in the little gray
hut; he never laughed himself as he did when he
was with Luigi and his brothers. Everything was
so solemn and quiet wherever Faustina was, that no
one would have dared to laugh, except, perhaps,
the little brooklet Ema, a saucy little stream that
cares for nothing as it ripples by to throw itself
into the arms of the Greve.[1]

[1] A small river.

Often and often, after a happy day in the city with Luigi, Raffaello would come back and feel even more conscious of the dreariness of his home, and he would resolve to ask Faustina about it, and beg her to tell him what was the cause of it, and whether there was anything he could do to help it. But he never had the courage to follow out this resolution; for it seemed that at those very times Faustina was more silent and gloòmy and forbidding than ever.

Many days went by, and he kept his little troubles to himself, having been admonished by Faustina that he must hold his tongue, and not talk of himself or of her to those young parrots, Luigi and his brothers, who had no more sense in their noddles than yellow pumpkins. He went to the city with them very often, nevertheless, and found them agreeable and kind companions in spite of what Faustina said; and those days were always *festa* days for him. He grew better acquainted with the big gray city, its little crooked streets, and its broad *piazzas;* and after that first day of his good-fortune, he was no longer afraid of holding up his flowers to the passers-by. He was so like a little flower himself that many stopped to look at the baby face, and bought of him, when they had driven away a dozen bolder vendors, and gave him twice what he asked for his

posies.   And so he grew to be a power in the house
with his little income of centimes, and soon was pay-
ing half the rent, though he was hardly seven years old.
   One day when Faustina had told him to buy himself a bun out of his money for his mid-day meal, as
she was going out and there would be no dinner
when he got back, the happy thought came to him
that he would buy something for her instead, and
take it home that night.   There happened to be
passing a noisy peddler with a most enticing tray
of trinkets suspended from his neck, — gilded rings
and brooches, and bits of red coral and blue tur-
quoise.   Raffaello eyed them wistfully, with a child's
love for bright things, and followed the man a little
way, feeling for his pennies in his little *scarsella*,[1]
when the peddler caught sight of him.
   "Oh, you pretty pigeon, what bright eyes you've
got, and what pretty curls !   Don't you want to give
me one of those lovely ringlets of yours in exchange
for some of my wares?   See these fine coral beads !
The blessed Mother would be mightily pleased if
you said your prayers to her on such a splendid
rosary as this.   It's a beauty !" and he dangled the
beauty in question with a most persuasive wink.
   " I should not like to part with my curls," said

[1] A sort of money-bag worn by the country-folk

Raffaello, " but I would give you some *quattrini* for the beads. I would like to buy them for Faustina."

"Santa Lucia! do you think you have got *quattrini* enough to buy these?" laughed the amused peddler. " Why, they are fine enough to give to the Pope himself! They are worth a fortune; you will never see as much money as it would take to buy them. Yet, I will let you have the beads for your curls."

He laid his hand caressingly on Raffaello's dark hair, thinking what a good bargain he could make of the soft silken ringlets with the wig-maker in his neighborhood; for this peddler was not unlike most peddlers in Italy, and never missed a chance of making a good trade, no matter whether it was in his line of business or not. But Raffaello was not inclined to favor this proposal; he did not feel that his curls were his own to give away, and Faustina had allowed him only the price of a bun, so he said timidly, —

" For how much would you sell them?"

" Suffocation! What a stupid *bimbo* you are! You will not give your curls? "

" I am afraid Faustina would not like it."

" A florin,[1] then! "

1 The largest of Florentine silver coins, worth about fifty cents.

" I know what sort of paste you are made of, you ! "

That was so much money that Raffaello drew
back, and eyed the small copper coins in his hand
with a disappointed look, while the peddler gave
a great shout of laughter at his discomfiture.

" Hold your noise, you braying donkey ! "
shouted a deep voice from across the way. " What
do you mean by parrying with a *bimbo* not a
quarter your size ! A bad digestion to you ! "

Raffaello looked up, — they were standing on a
corner of the Via Porta Rossa, near the Mercato
Nuovo,[1] — and he saw a large fat man, with a very
familiar face, and a recognizable glazed hat resting
indifferently on his left ear, sitting beside a vegetable stall shelling peas.

" Oh, it is you, Signor Camillo ! " cried Raffaello,
in pleasant surprise.

" Purgatory take me, if it is n't the good
bimbo ! " ejaculated the crimsoned-face *cocchiere.*
" What mischievous luck has brought you in company with that blear-eyed turnip of a peddler !
Ecco ! *I* know what sort of paste you are made of,
you ! " and he doubled up his fist at the man with
a significant thrust.

" *Altro ! Sor cocchiere,*[2] I was but jesting with the
youngster," said the peddler, apologetically ; " he 's

---

[1] The New Market. [2] Sir coachman.

such a pretty pigeon, and he's got such pretty
curls!" and again the large hand was stretched out
to stroke the coveted treasure.

"*Saperlotti!* keep your hands off him, will you!"
growled the infuriated Camillo, suddenly feeling a
certain proprietorship in the little boy, and flinging a
handful of empty shells at the too familiar tradesman.

"*Che, che,*" retorted the man. "I'm not going
to do him any harm!   Do you think I've got the
plague?"

"A plague on you for your impudence! Get
along with you, and your silly traffic; get along,
and break stones at Carrara, and leave the peddling
to the women and the children!" and Camillo's
face grew quite blue with indignation.

"Fie!" remonstrated the peddler, with a grimace.
"I'm only having a little game with the boy. What
have you got to say about it; he's not your *bimbo*,
is he?"

"Never you mind whose *bimbo* he is. If you
want to sell him the beads for what they are worth, —
which is n't half the price of this chestnut," and he
sent the brown missile dexterously at the peddler's
nose, — "sell them. If not, get along with you!"

All this was shouted back and forth across the
way, for the streets in that quarter of Florence are

so narrow that it is not worth one's while to cross
over to carry on a conversation, and by this time a
curious crowd had gathered to witness the fun, and
to urge the irate *cocchiere* with shouts of, " That's
it, Camillo! Roast him, roast him, to the ears!"

Camillo needed no urging, for he was in his
element whenever he saw a good opportunity for
" roasting " a fellow-creature. Everybody knew him
to be a match for all the other "cabbies " in the
city put together.

When Raffaello told him that he wished to purchase the red beads, he immediately entered into
the spirit of a bargain with cheerfulness. The
peddler, as a matter of course, asked a ridiculously
large sum for the rosary; and Camillo offered him
a ridiculously small one. The matter finally ended
in Raffaello's obtaining the pretty trinket for just
the price of his bun, and in his sharing the dinner
of the kind-hearted coachman, who felt it his
duty to reward the little boy for his generous
deed.

It was about noon, and he sat down on a low box
beside Camillo, at the latter's invitation, in front
of the vegetable stall, and waited until the owner of
the shop brought them a bowl of hot soup and a
square of bread. The owner of the shop was a

friend of Camillo's, — a man with a wooden leg and a pleasant face, — who was known as " Giojoso," in the neighborhood, because he was such a cheerful and amiable person.

" Is this where you live ? " inquired Raffaello of the *cocchiere.*

" No, no, *mignone;*[1] have you forgotten I told you that I lived behind the Badia, in a garret with the *madre* and the parrot? This is Giojoso's shop."

" Why do you shell peas here, instead of driving your splendid carriage ? " Raffaello ventured to ask ; for he could not understand why Camillo, who appeared to him a very grand and mighty personage, should be sitting at another man's door engaged in such a very trivial occupation.

" Well, you see, Raffaello *mio,*" said his fat friend, stretching his legs very far out in front of him, and nodding, as if he were about to tell him something very private and confidential, " we *cocchieri* are not a rich tribe; we 're a lot of miserable beggars, that 's what we are! That," and he pointed with his finger to the " splendid carriage " and the nag, which were stationed at a short distance from where he sat, — " why, what with these

[1] A pet name.

new-fangled omnibuses travelling all over the city
for a song, *that* hardly earns enough in one day
to buy a good meal at night for the *madre* and
the parrot. And when one has an old *madre* to
look after, one must look about for something
more to do during the idle moments. Giojoso,
here, is a good fellow; and in the warm season,
when the cooks are lazy, and want to buy their
peas already shelled, and their beans already
strung, I come here and sit, and shell the peas for
Giojoso; and he gives me my dinner for my pains,
and a bit of cheese and a handful of figs to take
home besides. Ho, ho, ho, Giojoso is a good
fellow; and may San Pietro help him up to Paradise!" cried the hearty Camillo, as he caught sight
of the wooden-leg ambling towards them, and then
of the steaming soup.

This was all rather mysterious to little Raffaello.
He watched his good-natured friend with renewed
interest, without being able to understand what it
was that made him so jolly, for he had said that
he was poor. Raffaello always fancied that it was
because they were so poor that Faustina grumbled
and scolded so much. Camillo was the drollest
person he had ever seen. He seemed to be always
laughing; even while he used his strongest language

with his adversary a moment ago, there had been
a smile lurking in every wrinkle of his good face.

"I like you very much, Camillo," said the child,
innocently, having suddenly come to that conclu-
sion, as he sat watching the great gulps of hot soup
that disappeared down Camillo's throat, "and I
wish I could see you often when I come to the
city."

"That's a bargain, *bimbo!*" cried the *cocchiere,*
chucking him under the chin. "Come right here
when you want to find me and my nag. We are
here every day at noon; and some day, when we are
not in a tremendous hurry, I will take you up to
see the *madre* and the parrot. Oh, they're a pair!
They talk at each other without taking any notice
of what the other says; and they quarrel like two
old roosters."

Raffaello thought that it would be very amusing
to hear the parrot talk; and he made up his mind
to take the first opportunity that was offered him,
of becoming better acquainted with Camillo, as the
simple old fellow went on to relate more of the
pleasures and delights of his home life.

There was a bright display of fresh vegetables
in front of Giojoso's shop, relieved here and there
with a touch of scarlet tomato and ruby-red rad-

ishes, and baskets of large rosy berries that were brought from Al Prato. Inside, there were dried figs and nuts, and sweet yellow butter, and creamy cheeses; and there was also a big white cat, not so large or so handsome as Minnetto, to be sure, and not so lazy either, for this one had a famous reputation for catching rats and mice; and the cheeses and the macaroni were as safe, when he was about, as if they had been in the Pope's coffers, so Giojoso said. Then, there was a very old blue and white Madonna over the door, with a small red oil-lamp burning under it night and day, and some queer faded old paintings on the sides of the wall. Raffaello made a mental note of all these things in Giojoso's little shop, before taking his leave, that he might be sure to find the place again when he returned the following week to see Camillo. Then he said good-bye to his new friends, thanking them heartily, and hurried away, hugging the precious beads, to meet Luigi and his brothers at the accustomed place.

When he showed the lovely rosary to Faustina that evening, she was not as gracious or as pleased as he had hoped. She mumbled something about his taste being much too fine for his purse, and said "what need had she of a coral rosary! The

Madonna had paid no heed to her prayers all these
years, as she said them over the black wooden
beads; did he think she would listen better if she
said them over the red ones?"

"I thought you would like them," said Raffaello,
feeling a little disappointed, though if he had been
older and wiser, he would have known that it was
Faustina's habit never to seem pleased with anything. "Luigi's mother has some corals, and I
wanted you to have some too."

"Humph!" grumbled Faustina, "you are a silly
bimbo for giving away your money for such a
trinket. How much did you pay for it?"

Raffaello told her, and also that he had met the
jolly *cocchiere*, who had invited him to share his
dinner after the purchase was concluded. Faustina
had not the heart to express any further disapproval
when she learned that the gift had been bought
with the few cents she had told him to spend for
his meal. So she said nothing more; but she laid
the beads carefully away in the locked box, beside
the little gold medal, as if she considered them
something very precious.

Chapter VI

SUMMER was now gone, and the lovely autumn had taken its place. Florence was not much changed in the six months that had passed since the joyful feast of the Pasqua. The yellow Arno was only a little darker with reflections of the deepening autumn hues upon the surrounding landscape; but its swift, silent course was the same. The gray mass of old palaces was not more hoary; the fair towers rising up against the clouds were not less fair, as they looked down in all their majesty upon the changeless city. For what are six months to a city that has stood six hundred years? — a city whose temples, and towers, and palaces have only turned a little grayer as each generation of men has passed away and left them

standing there, immovable, like fair symbols of
eternity; a city whose every street-stone could tell
a story of the great mysterious past, whose every
bell, as it rings out upon the evening stillness, is
singing the praises of its great and glorious dead.
To a city like Florence, years are nothing.

But to a little boy like Raffaello the short space
of six months often makes a great change in his
life. Raffaello had grown, in those few months,
to know and love the beautiful old city, and to
feel happiest when he was wandering about its
narrow streets, or sitting quiet in one of its vast
silent churches, where the people came and knelt
a few moments on their various ways. He thought
a great deal in those days, for he was just reaching
the age when little folk wonder at the things
they see, and like to ask questions about them.
Raffaello knew very few people with whom he felt
free enough to ask questions: of Faustina, he
would not dare; of Minnetto it would be of no
use, because Minnetto was such a conservative
old creature that he never committed himself
by words. There was really no one but Camillo,
the *cocchiere*, and Raffaello found endless pleasure
in his weekly visits to the old fellow. He always
came away with a higher opinion of the coachman's

knowledge; for Camillo knew everybody, and everything that had happened in his generation. He knew the city like a book, and he helped Raffaello to find his way, taught him the names of the streets and churches, showed him the places most frequented by the great and rich people, and had even told him the names of some of them.

As long as the season lasted, Camillo held his post at the vegetable stall, and shelled peas and strung beans for Giojoso of the wooden leg, and earned his dinner thereby; and he lost no chance of quarrelling with the passers-by, or of entering into a dispute with those who came there to market. But he was always kind to little Raffaello, and in time grew very fond of him.

But now that the summer was gone, and the rainy days were beginning, and people did not enjoy walking about in the wet, Camillo's own business grew more thriving, and Raffaello did not see him quite so often. So he took to going into the churches through the day to rest and spend what time he had left, quietly looking at the old frescos on the walls, and at the bright-colored window-glass, and the strange waxen images of the saints in the little chapels.

It happened to be on the feast of All Saints,

that autumn, that Raffaello first strayed into the old *piazza* of Santissima Annunziata. This was one of the few places where he had not been, and his attention was immediately drawn to the old portico of the church, where numbers of people were going in with wreaths of immortelles to lay at some altar, in memory of their dear ones. It was after twelve o'clock, and the masses were over. Raffaello followed the crowds through the little court-yard that leads into the church. There were many worshippers there still, of all sorts and classes of people; for the Annunziata is open to all on feast days, though ordinarily it is the place where the nobility go to worship. Some were telling their beads, others were laying their wreaths at the foot of the altars, others were sitting on low stools in prayerful meditation; others, feeling strange, like little Raffaello, were looking about at people, and wondering at the vastness of those great aisles in which the multitude seemed to lose itself as soon as it entered. As Raffaello stood near the steps of one of the little side-chapels, which is the shrine of Saint Joseph, the patron saint of all little children, he noticed a very tall old gentleman, with long white hair and a thin white face, who was kneeling at this altar. Very near him was a young

" He clasped his hands and fell on his knees before her."

girl who also knelt and prayed. She was dressed in white, and her rich dark hair fell over her shoulders. Her hands were clasped and her head bowed, and Raffaello could see her clear fine profile delicately outlined against the dark wall of the chapel. It was a beautiful face, gentle, pious, and womanly, though it was very young, of that delicate texture and coloring that is seen only among the high-born and high-bred people of that country.

The light of the tall wax candles fell upon her and shed such a lustre on her rich hair that it shone all about her head like an aureole; and Raffaello thought she must be one of the lovely painted saints, until she rose and turned away from the altar, and gave her hand to the old man. As they passed, the edge of her white dress softly brushed Raffaello's cheek. He clasped his hands and fell on his knees before her. But she did not see him; she was helping the old *signor* down the two or three steps, and whispering words of comfort in his ear, though her own beautiful eyes were tearful, and her lips trembled as she spoke.

" *Dio mio!* " whispered little Raffaello under his breath, " it is an angel!" and he watched them walking slowly down the aisle until the two figures had disappeared behind the heavy door.

The moment the bright vision was gone, Raffaello felt a vague sense of loneliness, as if he had suddenly lost something very dear. Child-like, he followed his first impulse, which was to go out after them and look again at the beautiful face. When he reached the portico, the old gentleman was already seated in an elegant closed carriage which bore a rich monogram on the door, and was drawn by two handsome horses. She was standing on the edge of the walk, giving charities to a number of ragged-looking children that stood around. Raffaello would have gone nearer, just to receive one glance from her sweet dove-like eyes, except for the dread he had of being thought a beggar. He stood a little hidden behind one of the arches of the portico, and saw her re-enter the carriage, and take her place beside the white-haired old man.

They drove across to the left of the square, and stopped in front of the old Foundling's Hospital, the oldest in Florence, where the great Lucca della Robia's famous "infants in swaddling-clothes" still adorn the tops of its low stone arches. Raffaello saw a man come out of the door of the hospital and hold a box to the window of the carriage, and again he saw the beautiful *signorina* [1] as she leaned out

---

[1] Young lady.

and dropped some large gold pieces in the box. Then they turned down into the via della Colonna, and the big horses went so fast that Raffaello soon lost sight of them.

Who was she; and where were the horses running away with her so fast, so fast? What was it that had made his little hands grow cold, and his cheeks burn when he had caught sight of her face; that made him feel sad now that she was gone; that made him wish he could have known her and loved her like the dear Madonna to whom he prayed with childish faith, but who seemed always so very far away?

Raffaello had never before seen any one who made him feel like this. He had seen many pretty faces and great ladies at the Mercato Nuovo on a Thursday morning, buying flowers; but he had never seen a face just like hers. It was so sweet and so sad, as if some sorrow had already shadowed her bright young beauty. He had no more rest, now; his young and quick imagination began at once to weave a web of golden fancies about the fair *signorina*. That night, as he and Minnetto were sitting close together beside the kitchen fire, he took the sleepy creature into his confidence.

" Minnetto," he whispered, putting his lips close

to the fidgeting ear of the cat, " I have seen to-day
the most beautiful *signorina* in the world! "

Minnetto looked from the fire to Raffaello, and
the pupils of his big yellow eyes were like two long
exclamation points, with the air of one who should
say, " Well, indeed ! and what of that, you pretty,
silly *bimbo?* "

" Oh, but you don't know, Minnetto, how lovely
she is; you have never seen any one like her. She
has a face like an angel's, and her eyes are like
those of the painted Madonna above the altar of
San Gaggio. I saw her at the church this morning, and I know she is a great lady, for she rides in
a grand carriage, and she gives money to the poor.
I shall ask Camillo about her when I see him.
Camillo knows everybody ; he will know about her,
and perhaps he will tell me where I may go and
see her again. And if you are such a lazy, bad
pussy, Minnetto, you will never see her," said
Raffaello, playfully frowzling the big head.

For Minnetto, who, as I have said before, was not
a sympathetic listener, had by this time found his
accustomed place in the hollow of Raffaello's elbow,
and was purring and snoozing contentedly.

CHAPTER VII

THE next time Raffaello was in the city, he went in search of Camillo at his own dwelling behind the Badia. It was several weeks since he had seen his good friend, and he could stand the separation no longer. Besides, he might not be going to Florence every week, now that the flowers were all gone, and Luigi and his brothers would not be using the cart any more; for Pierrota was getting so old and so unreasonable that it was easier for the two elder lads to walk the distance than to try to make any amicable arrangement with the donkey for going quietly and peaceably on her way.

It was late in the afternoon when Raffaello knocked at the door of the little garret of one of the old stone houses in the Via Condotta. He had climbed so many crooked winding steps to reach the top that he was obliged to stop to catch his breath before lifting the big iron knocker.

"Who's there?" said a strange, sharp, croaking voice from within.

Raffaello timidly gave his name.

"Who are you?" asked the voice, with a very unmusical laugh. "Come in, stay out! ha, ha, ha! you ugly old bird;" and then there was a sound of much fluttering and bumping and scratching, and more croaking, as if a flock of owls had been suddenly let loose in the room.

Raffaello hesitated about accepting this doubtful invitation, which had come from the parrot, when a key turned in the lock, and the door opened just a small crack, for it was held from the inside by a loose chain. A very withered old woman appeared behind the crack, and Raffaello judged she must be Camillo's mother. The old woman was very deaf, and he did not succeed very well in making her understand that he was come to see Camillo. But the parrot, who always acted as interpreter between any strangers and the old lady, and whose voice was more piercing than Raffaello's, jumped on her shoulder and screamed in her ear, "Camillo! Camillo! You ugly old bird! ha, ha, ha!"

"Hold your tongue, you saucy brute!" returned the *madre*, as she loosened the chain with shaking fingers, and beckoned Raffaello to come in. The

old woman looked at her little visitor with some
curiosity, and mumbled something which Raffaello
could not make out.   Evidently Camillo had never
mentioned his little friend at home, which was not
surprising, for it was impossible to converse intelli-
gently with the old mother without rousing the
whole neighborhood, and, perforce, taking them all
into his confidence.   And since he had become better
acquainted with the little boy, Camillo had especial
reasons for keeping his interest in him quiet.

The *madre* was kind to Raffaello, and gave him a
little stool to sit on, and asked him to wait till
Camillo came in, which would be very soon.   For,
like the good son that he was, Camillo always made
it a point of running in between his trips, several
times through the day, to see how his family were
faring.

"You're a pretty *bimbo*," she said, laying her
hand on his curls, though she could not see him
well, her eyes being old and worn out.

"A pretty *bimbo!* ha, ha, ha, what lies!" shrieked
the parrot.

"Don't mind that stupid creature, he's a hideous
old crow," said the *madre*, making as if she would
give the parrot a whack with her stick, though she
had not the least idea of what he was saying.

"A hideous old crow!" interrupted the saucy bird.

"He's the bane of my life, he's so ugly and he shrieks so; a person would think I was deaf! I'll wring your neck for you, you old torment, if you don't stop your noise!"

The parrot was walking up and down the room, bridling and sidling up to the old woman with the most provoking impudence, cocking his green eye on one side, and saying every now and then, "Get along, you old fright!"

Raffaello thought that the parrot was a very daring bird, and not very polite; but he was certainly very droll, especially when he began pecking at the old lady's toes, and she made at him with her stick; while he flew off to his perch, screaming, "Murder! murder! glory be to Peter!"

It was a gloomy, dingy little room, in spite of the liveliness that went on there between the old *madre* and the parrot. It being immediately under the roof, the ceilings were crooked and slanting, and Raffaello could see, from one of the low, narrow windows, the tops of all the high buildings on the sunny side of Florence, and bits of gardens on the roofs of other dwellings, and people's clothes hanging out to dry on lines stretched across from house

"Get along, you old fright!"

to house, and women, babies, and cats looking out of windows. And looking down, down into the narrow streets and courts below, the people there seemed to Raffaello no bigger than dwarfs. He felt very much like one of the pigeons of the Uffizzi, as he looked out of that small opening; and he wondered how the people here could live contentedly in those high, dreary places, without ever getting a breath of the pure, fresh air of the open country, or the sweet scent of the new-mown grass, and with only a small patch of sky above them to look at.

The room itself was bare enough, but in this respect it was not unlike Faustina's house. The floor was laid with bricks, and there was no such thing as a carpet or rug of any description on its chill surface. There was not even a fire in the small earthen brazier which stood in the hollow of the chimney, and which was lighted and kept going with a few bits of charcoal only when it was neces-sary to cook a meal, although it was already far into November. But the *madre* wore a flannel shawl over head and shoulders to keep her warm when she was not chasing the parrot for exercise, and Coco, the bird, had a nice warm coat of green and yellow feathers, and did not seem to mind the cold a particle. There was a round table in the centre of the room spread with an oil-cloth, and a few wooden chairs, and an old cupboard with only one door, from which the *madre* soon began to take some things to make the table ready for Camillo's coming. It was growing late, and past the hour when Raffaello should have been hastening to meet Luigi and the cart to return to the village; but he was so interested in his surroundings, and in his desire to see Camillo and talk with him about the beautiful *signorina*, that he quite forgot the time of day.

It was not long before some one came puffing up the narrow stairs, singing a joyful too-loo-rool, that was very suggestive of the master of the house. A tremendous pounding resounded on the knocker, which even the old *madre* heard, and presently the beaming face of the good *cocchiere* appeared in the door.

"Cristoforo Colombo!" he roared, as soon as he caught sight of little Raffaello. "Why, *mignone*, you're as welcome as hot macaroni and cheese! What's brought you here; not in trouble, eh?"

"Oh, no!" said Raffaello, "I wanted very much to see you. I have been several times to Giojoso's shop to find you; but Giojoso said you were very busy, and did not come around any more."

"Giojoso is right, I have been busy of late," said Camillo, with a very mysterious winking of one eye. "I have been studying some ancient history."

"I remembered that you said you lived behind the Badia," continued Raffaello, "and I thought you would not mind if I came to see you here."

"Mind? you little pigeon! Have n't I said that the sight of your pretty face is as good as Lourdes [1] water for the eyes! And how have they used you, the *madre* and the parrot?"

"Oh, very kindly," said Raffaello, glancing at the old dame, who was now very busy warming some soup that had onions and parsley in it, and sent out the most savory vapors.

"That's well," rejoined Camillo. "The *madre* is always kind; but the parrot is a beast!"

"You'll never die, ha, ha, ha!" squalled the parrot, descending from his perch to tweak one of Raffaello's curls, with whom he was beginning to feel familiar.

"Silence! or *you'll* die, you ugly monster!" shouted Camillo, bouncing upon him, and giving his tail a series of jerks as if it had been a door-bell. "I'll crack your stupid skull as quick as I would the claw of a lobster!"

[1] Water from a fountain in Southern France, which is supposed to cure the blind.

It was a good thing for the Tuscan Polly that his nature was not a sensitive one; for each time he interrupted the conversation, he was rebuffed in the same unmistakable terms by Camillo or the *madre*, and was threatened with a multitude of tortures which neither of them had the least intention of carrying out.

"And so you remembered that I lived behind the Badia," resumed Camillo, in a presto change of tone, "and that my number is — ? "

"Twenty-one," said Raffaello.

"Good!" exclaimed the delighted coachman. "A *bimbo* who does not forget his old friend, or his old friend's number, even when that old friend is a beggar of a *cocchiere*, — that *bimbo*, I say, ought to have a good treat, and a treat he shall have; for the *madre's* soup of beans is the best to be had in Florence!" and he drew the little wooden stool on which Raffaello sat, close to the table, and took his own place beside him.

It was such a new thing to Raffaello to have some one talk pleasantly to him, and take a friendly interest in him, that he felt quite happy whenever he was in Camillo's company. Faustina never treated him as if she thought him of any more consequence than the cat. She never called him a good *bimbo*, or a pretty pigeon, or showed him in any way that she was fond of him; and yet he would rather have had that from her than anything else she could do for him. For children have great need of kindness, especially when their own nature is gentle and loving. Little Raffaello was instinctively drawn to this big, hearty, good-natured man, in spite of his loud, though not very dangerous bark, and his rough and red exterior. Indeed, he felt a certain security in having Camillo for his friend and protector; and his admiration for and confidence in the old fellow's opinion on almost every subject, were boundless.

Under the genial influence of the *madre's* good soup and Camillo's broad smiling face, Raffaello grew quite talkative, and even confidential. He related how he had been to the Annunziata on the feast of Ogni Santi, and there had seen the beautiful *signorina* and the white-haired old *signor;* how they had knelt at the foot of the altar, and left a wreath of white flowers for Saint Joseph; and how sad the *signorina* looked, and how he had thought of her every day, and dreamed of her every night since. Then he asked, with a wistful look in his big soft eyes, —

"Do you know where she lives, Camillo, and

where I may go and look at her again? I have
searched for her every time I have been in the
city, but I have never seen her face but that once, —
not at the church, nor at the market where the
great ladies come to buy flowers every Thursday,
not anywhere. And so I thought perhaps you
could tell me, for you surely know everybody who
lives in Florence, don't you, Camillo?"

Camillo had been listening very attentively, and
very quietly for him, while the little boy was speak-
ing. His mouth was screwed up mysteriously, his
eyes were partly closed, and there was a great
wrinkle across his forehead, all of which gave him
such an air of wisdom and secrecy that Raffaello
felt encouraged.

"Well," said the *cocchiere*, draining the last drop
of soup from his bowl, "Camillo knows nearly everybody. If there is anybody worth knowing that he
does n't know, it won't be long before he finds them
out. *Ecco!* what is a coachman good for, if he
does n't know his city like his own pocket?"

Here the parrot chimed in, "Good for nothing,
good for nothing, you old rooster!" whereupon
Camillo threatened to tear out his heart and liver,
in parenthesis, and then resumed amiably, —

"And you say the *signorina* is beautiful?"

"Just like an angel!" cried Raffaello, warmly.

"And young? about how young, now?"

"I don't know," answered Raffaello, puzzled; "but she is nearly as tall as the old man, for he is bent, and stoops over when he walks; and she wears a white dress that comes down to her feet, like the ladies I have seen in the gardens of the palaces; but her face is like that of the Babe in the Madonna's arms."

"And what color are her eyes?" inquired Camillo.

"Big and black," — for he had treasured every feature of the fair face, in that one glance when she had passed so close to him in the church.

"And they ride in a splendid coach, with something marked on the door?"

"Yes, a little crown of yellow, and something like this underneath it;" and Raffaello traced out the imperfect and distorted outline of a capital B with his spoon upon the oil-cloth.

"And you say they turned down the Via della Colonna?"

"Yes, after giving something at the hospital."

"*Che, che*, Raffaellino! they belong to the great *signori*, you may be sure of that. Whenever you see a crown on a coach-door, those who ride in it are none of your common *popoli* who barter with a poor beggar of a coachman like me for a *soldo* more

or a *soldo* less!   Now, you don't see any crown on
my cab, do you, Raffaellino?   *Altro !* that's what
comes of being put into the world on the side
where the *scudi*[1] are raining!" and Camillo
laughed long and loud at the idea, as if it were an
immensely amusing one.

Little Raffaello had never thought of drawing any
comparisons between the *signorina's* splendid equipage and the humble public conveyance with which
Camillo earned his living; but he laughed too,
simply because Camillo was laughing, without being
in absolute possession of the joke.

"If you should be near the Annunziata on a
Sunday," suggested Raffaello, "perhaps you would
like to stop in the *piazza*, and watch for her to
come out of the church.   I should love to have
you see her, Camillo."

"What a sly little rabbit!" and the *cocchiere*
laughed again.   "What do you think will come of
it, if I do see your lovely *signorina ?*   Do you think
she will stop me on the street to ask me if I know
any pretty *bimbo* with a face like a peach-blossom,
who would like to come and be her page, and walk
behind her, and carry her fan, and pick up her
kerchief, and admire her the livelong day ? "

[1] Gold coins.

This was a daring and dangerous suggestion for Camillo to make, for immediately Raffaello's eyes lighted up, and he cried eagerly, " Oh, do great ladies ever have little boys come and stay with them like that?" and a vague thought flashed through his mind of how it would seem to leave Faustina and Minnetto and the little hut, and go where he could always look at the beautiful lady.

" Ah, well, they do it sometimes," said Camillo; "but we must not think of that now. Some day, I will find out all about the *signorina* and tell you; but it may not be for a long time, for I am a man of business these days, and have n't many spare hours to go loitering around the church to see pretty faces coming out of it!" And Camillo made light of the matter, as if he did not mean to give it much thought; but he did. With his usual aptitude for unravelling any sort of mystery that chanced in his way, he added this little circumstance to some other facts which he had been treasuring in his own mind for some time, and feeling that he had just made another cunning discovery, he slapped his knee and repeated now and then, " Camillo, you 're as sly as an old eel!"

In the midst of this, the deep tones of a neighboring bell broke in upon them. There had been a short pause after Camillo's last speech.

"What is that?" asked Raffaello, startled out of his reverie, for the sound was very near.

"It is the bell of the Badia striking the seventh hour," said Camillo.

"Oh, is it so very late? I did not know it; I am afraid Luigi will have gone, and I must walk back to the village! And Faustina, oh, she will be so frightened! she will think I am lost!" cried little Raffaello, in dismay. For while they sat conversing, he had not thought of the time, and had not noticed that it was quite dark in the little garret-room now; for the sun had sunk very low, and the hills around the city were darkening.

"San Pietro! It is late for a little *contadino* to be in town. We have been chattering like two magpies, and letting the hours run by. But never fear; you will not have to walk to the village. It would take your little legs so long that Faustina would think the locusts had eaten you on the way. No, the nag is downstairs, waiting at the door. I will take you at once to the *piazza*, and if Luigi is gone, then we will stretch our ride a little further and take you home. The nag likes nothing better than a turn in the country after trotting on hard stones all day; and her legs are so good that we will pass Pierrota and Luigi on the way, and be the first ones there."

This was very comforting to poor Raffaello, who had begun to be really frightened at the thought of having missed his little companions and having to go that long distance in the dark alone. But Camillo was such a good friend! He was always getting the little boy out of his troubles.

So they hurried away on the box of Camillo's coach to the cathedral-square, where, seeing no sign of Luigi, or of the cart and Pierrota, they speedily made their way to the Porta Romana, and were soon on their way to Galluzzo.

This was how Camillo came to make his first acquaintance with Faustina. When they reached the little hut, he, of course, took all the blame of the little boy's tardiness upon himself; and told such funny stories, and made himself so thoroughly agreeable to Faustina, who was really very grateful for the safe return of the child, that she did not utter one cross word or reproach, and was kinder to Raffaello that evening than she had ever been before.

CHAPTER VIII

RAFFAELLO did not go any more into the city for the rest of that year. The winter set in unusually cold, and no one cared to face the bleak, chill wind that blew over from the distant mountains, unless he was obliged to do so. The people in the village of Galluzzo were very much like ants who work all summer to fill up their store-houses and shut themselves up, never putting their noses out, during the wintry season. I do not mean that all the village people were as thrifty and as wise as the frugal ant, for many of them suffered bitterly on account of their improvidence when the cold weather came. They had hard work, at best, to live in their miserable quarters, and might have perished but for the help of their more prudent neighbors. But those who had been wise enough to lay up provisions against the bad days, kept within doors, and left the cold weather and the rest of the world to take care of themselves.

Faustina was one of those who had been prudent, and now she and Raffaello and the cat lived more secluded and alone than ever. It was very hard for the little boy to spend whole days in the dingy hut, with only Faustina, who sat knitting and grumbling, and Minnetto, who lay napping and purring, and with only the wail of the wind calling dismally through the chimney instead of Camillo's hearty laugh; and only the gray outlook of the barren hills and naked trees, instead of the smiling, flowery welcome of the lovely city, as he had seen it first that day in the early spring-time. He began to hate the winter, and to long for the return of summer. If he had never known that joyous freedom, he would have been no worse off than he was the year before at that time; he would have gone on gathering wood for Faustina to burn, and milking the goat, and fetching the grain from the mill, and never dreamed of any other life. But now that his experience had been so widened, that he knew the delights of the city, had met Camillo; now that he had seen the beautiful *signorina!* Ah, now, indeed,

it was very different. He felt sometimes as if he
could never wait through those long, long days, and
sit through those dreary, cold evenings, until the
happy spring was come again, when he might seek
the places and the people that he loved.

One evening when he and Minnetto sat beside
the kitchen hearth where the fire had been, but was
now only a heap of black ashes, Raffaello thought:

"Only a little while ago the twigs were burning
and crackling and sending out their warmth as if
they were happy, and now they are all black and
cold and look dead, and must stay so until Faustina
lights the fire again to-morrow to warm the milk.
That is like me; a few weeks ago I was in Florence,
and the sun was warm, and the flowers were bright,
and I was with Camillo and the *madre*, and I saw
the lovely lady; and now, everything is gray and
cold and gloomy there, and I must stay in this little
hut until the good God lights the fire in the big sun
again, and makes us all warm and happy."

He gave a sigh that sounded so loud in the stillness of the little room, that Minnetto opened his
sleepy eyes for a moment, and looked at him inquir-
ingly. Faustina sat beside the table with her work
in her lap. She did not look up when she heard
the sigh; she was looking at him already. She had

been watching him all the evening, as he sat on his
little straw cushion, at a short distance from her,
holding his knees. The light of the one candle fell
full on his face. It was a very thoughtful little face
His large dark eyes had a look in them that smote
Faustina's heart. She would have said something
kind to turn his thoughts to her; but she could not.
Habit is so very strong in people; and it had been
her habit for many years to speak no kind word to
any one. Now, as she watched the fair young face,
and guessed that he was thinking of things about
which she dared not ask, she would have given
worlds to draw him to her, and gain his confidence;
but she had not a single word to win him. She felt
a great deal for him; but like all hard, undemonstra-
tive natures, she did not know how to show all she
felt. In the bitterness of her revengeful feeling,
she had taught herself to scoff at every tender emotion; and her heart, instead of being a sensitive
human thing, full of sweet sympathy, was like a
hard shell.

She watched little Raffaello until she thought the
sight of him, looking so pensive and pitiful, would
drive her mad. Then she said suddenly, and in her
usual harsh tones, —

" What are you doing there, thinking all evening,

and never opening your mouth any more than the cat? You don't think I am good enough to talk to, perhaps, now you've got your fine friends in the city!"

"Oh, no, Faustina, it is not that," replied Raffaello, surprised by her sudden breaking of the silence. "I would indeed like to talk to you, if you did not mind my doing it. There are so many things I want to know."

"What things?" asked Faustina, sharply.

"Things about myself. I have often wanted to ask you why I never had any mother and father, and how you happened to take me to live with you."

Faustina took her eyes away from him, and looked at her work irresolutely; then she said, after a pause, —

"I found you."

"Found me!" repeated Raffaello, in great surprise.

"Yes, found you."

"Where?" inquired Raffaello.

"Never mind where," returned Faustina. "It's enough that I found you when you were a *bambinetto*, and cared for you, and fed you; and now it's a pretty reward I get for my pains: you want

to turn against me like all the rest of the world, and
you would like to find your fine father and mother,
who never so much as troubled themselves to come
to Galluzzo to find you ! "

Faustina spoke desperately. The thought that
Raffaello might wish to leave her to go to others,
stung her with disappointment. True, she had
never tried to make him love her; but she had
suffered much and endured much, in secret, for his
sake. Raffaello did not know this.

The little boy glanced at her curiously as she
spoke. He could not understand it all at once;
but the one thing that his sensitive nature did
understand, was that Faustina was hurt. He went
and stood beside her, and timidly put his hand on
her knee, and said as gently as he knew how, —

" Indeed, Faustina, I never wished to turn against
you, or to give you pain. You have been very
good to me. If you could only love me a little
more, and be happy, I am sure I should never ask
you about my father and mother, or think about
them."

Faustina pushed aside the candle and laid her
head on the table and covered her face with her
hands. It was eighteen years since she had shed
a tear; but there was an unconscious reproach in

Raffaello's last words that touched her, and she felt the justice of them. For one moment, the ice in her heart melted, and she wept. Raffaello felt terribly grieved. Forgetting her harsh words and her indifferent treatment of him, forgetting his own thoughts and hopes that he had cherished but a moment ago, forgetting everything save that she was in trouble, instinctively his arm stole about her neck, and he laid his soft round cheek against her hard one, and whispered, —

" Dear Faustina, don't cry, please. I want you to be happy, and when I am older I want to take care of you, and give you all you need, and be good to you, as you have been to me."

" Ah, Raffaello *mio*," said Faustina, " but that will not make me happy any more than I have made you happy. People can be happy with very little in this world, if they only have plenty of love; without that there is no happiness anywhere. God has taken away all those that I loved; he will take you away, too, when the time comes; so where is the use of my loving you, or your caring for me?"

Raffaello did not fully grasp the true wisdom of these words; but he knew better than she could tell him that there was something lacking in his feeling for her. He did not feel towards Faustina, with whom he had lived always, as he felt towards the beautiful *signorina* whom he had seen just once, as she knelt in the church. There was a hungry yearning in his young soul, that Faustina could never fill, even if she had suddenly turned very kind and gentle to him. Yet he was desperately sorry to see her thus; he would have preferred that she had scolded him or sent him off to his bed.

But Faustina did not send him off this time. The tears had washed some of her bitterness away, and she allowed him to remain near her a long time; but she did not say anything more.

As for Raffaello, he was more perplexed about himself than ever. Faustina had found him, and his parents had never come to look for him. Perhaps they had not cared about him any more than Faustina did; but this was a sad thought. Luigi's mother cared very much for him and his brothers; even Camillo and the *madre* were very fond of each other; and he had often seen mothers with little children in their arms, kissing and fondling them. Why was it so different with him? Camillo was really the only person who seemed to be very fond of Raffaello; ever since that day when he had first

run up against the big *cocchiere*, in front of the
Duomo, Camillo had been his friend, and had
always spoken kindly to him, and made much of
him. But now even Camillo seemed to have deserted him, for it was many weeks since he had
seen or heard of his old friend, and it was long past
the Christmas-tide.

It was just when Raffaello was pondering over all
this, still standing close to Faustina as she sat with
her head resting on the table, that they were both
roused by a sudden loud knock at the door of the
hut. They were startled at first, for a visitor at
any time was an unusual thing, and at that hour
of the night was unheard of. Before Faustina
could get to the door to unlatch it, the knock was
repeated with even more force; and when Faustina
opened it, who should burst in, with a merry and
hearty laugh, but Camillo himself, whose broad
genial face was like a sunbeam in the middle of
the night!

Raffaello gave a joyful cry and ran to him, saying,
" Oh, Camillo, where have you been ? I have not seen
you for so long !" Whereupon the jovial *cocchiere*
caught the little fellow in his arms and tossed him
up to the ceiling, with a cheery, " Ho, ho, *bambinetto!*
I have been studying ancient history," and restored

him to his feet again. After that, he extended his large palm to Faustina, and wished her a "*Buon appetito!*" which means a good appetite, and was really not very appropriate, for they had finished their supper long ago. But Camillo never stopped at such a small thing as that; he was full of good feeling and good news, and he could not begin to talk soon enough, though Faustina looked at him a little suspiciously, and was not very encouraging at first.

"You will excuse me for coming at this late hour, Monna Faustina," he said, with a beautiful bow, and a wink of one eye, which was his extremest mode of showing respect. "But good news is like cream; it will not keep over night without turning sour."

"Good news?" asked Faustina, incredulously, "for us!"

"*Ecco!* as good as the angel Gabriel himself could bring. I tell you, my good woman, it's a precious piece of luck for this young rabbit here!" and he laid his rough hand gently on Raffaello's curls.

Faustina turned white. She was always fearful of every little incident that came into their quiet lives, lest it might prove to be the very thing by which she should lose Raffaello. She felt that he would be taken from her sometime. She had said so to herself a great many times; she had said it to the little boy that night. He did not rightfully belong to her. She had hidden him away from every one as long as she could; but now he was grown beyond her, and he would soon be found out. For that reason, she could not help feeling doubtful and suspicious of any stranger who seemed to take any interest in him.

"Well?" said she, after a pause, during which Camillo had been winking and nodding and gesticulating mysteriously for Raffaello's benefit. "And what is your good news, *Sor cocchiere?* It is well you brought it, for it might have felt a stranger in this neighborhood, if it had come alone; there is little enough that's good ever finds its way here!"

"*Che, che*, Monna Faustina! You speak as if you had eaten too much pepper-weed. But you will be as sweet as honey when I tell you what rare good fortune has befallen this young cherub. Look at him!" and again he smoothed Raffaello's hair, "you who talk of nothing good ever finding its way here; did n't *he* come to you? Look at him, and tell me if there is another such a cherub-face outside of canvas!"

Faustina did not look at Raffaello, whose face was

delicately flushed and whose big eyes were bright
with expectation.   She was anxiously watching
Camillo.

"That's where your good fortune lies, friend
Faustina," continued the coachman, with growing
animation, and pointing straight at Raffaello. "Any
of our young artists would pay a fine sum for such
a model as that to paint from; and sitting for them
is a pleasanter task than digging turnips this cold
weather, let me tell you; it's only a matter of keeping still and looking pretty for an hour or two each
day; and that's easy enough for those who can do
it!   Though I could bet you an artichoke that
some of us would feel like sour crabs at it;" and
Camillo laughed such a tremendous laugh at his
own joke that he woke Minnetto out of a sound
sleep.   "Now, I know one Mariotto who is on the
search for just such a *bimbo*," pursued Camillo, as
no one chose to interrupt him in his disclosures, "to
put in his picture.   It is the picture of an angel
leading a little child; I have seen it.   The angel is
good; but the child, oh, Santa Lucia! he makes a
new face for it every day, and can never get in the
right one.   He is painting it for a rich old *signor*
who has a thousand notions, and is as hard to please
as the Pope himself; but he will pay a fortune to

the man who paints the right sort of face on that *bimbo*."

Camillo looked about to see what effect his remarks had produced on the little company. Raffaello's round eyes were still fastened on him, and Faustina only opened her mouth to say hoarsely, —

"Well?"

"Well, I told Mariotto that I knew a cherub whose face would surely do for the picture; and he said : ' Bring him to me if his eyes are dark and hand-some enough, and have a look in them like those of the Holy Infant in the Madonna's arms, and if his cheeks are the color of rose-petals, and his mouth makes a pure arch like that of a young moon; then, bring him to me, and I will make his fortune.' Now, Monna Faustina, if you do not call that the biggest handful of cherries that ever dropped into your lap, then I 'm a noodle, that 's all!" and Camillo lay back in his chair, and tumbled up his hair in a rakish fashion, and puffed out his red cheeks like two balloons, with the satisfied air of one who has just delivered himself of some very grave business. "What do you think of the proposition?" he asked, crossing his hands on his broad waistcoat, and leering archly at Faustina.

"Do you mean that I should let Raffaello go and sit to the painter every day?"

"Every day but Sunday and the *festas*, till the picture is finished," said Camillo; "and come back every night with a bright round silver *lira* in his pocket."

"We are poor," said Faustina, with a touch of her old pride in her tones, "and six *liras* in the week do not come often in the way of people like us; but if Raffaello wants to go and sit for the painter he may; and Mariotto can keep his *liras*, but he must paint me Raffaello's face, and give it to me for my very own to keep."

Camillo could scarcely repress his admiration of Faustina as she said this. He looked straight at her, and she looked straight at him; and he saw something in her eyes that made him take her hand and exclaim heartily, —

"Well done! Well said! you are a brave woman, Faustina, and you shall have your reward. I promise you the picture from Mariotto. And now that my beast has had time to rest his bones, I must be hurrying home to the *madre*. You will come to me to-morrow morning, Raffaello *mio*?"

"Oh, yes!" cried Raffaello, overjoyed at the prospect of renewing his visits to the city and to the good Camillo.

"And now, *A rivedello!*[1] and pleasant dreams to you both!" and the good *cocchiere* waved his hand to them, and bounced out as cheerily as he had bounced in; while Faustina and the boy stood at the door, candle in hand, to light him on his way.

[1] Good-bye.

CHAPTER IX

"SO," thought Raffaello, as he lay on his little straw bed that night, "the dear, good Camillo did not forget me after all; for he thought of me when the painter wanted somebody to put in his picture, and took the trouble to come all the way from the city so late at night to tell us about it!" and the little boy felt comforted and hopeful once more. For the mere sight of the big coachman, with his broad smiles and genial voice, was enough to drive away even sadder thoughts than those which Raffaello had entertained earlier in the evening.

Indeed, nothing could be farther from Camillo's thoughts than forgetting the little friend, in whom he had taken such lively interest and around whom he had already woven such a veil of pleasant possibilities, after his own ingenious fashion. Camillo had declared to himself, and had frequently offered to bet several artichokes with himself, that this pretty *bimbo* with a face like a picture was none of your common street-tribe, and that there was some mystery about him, which Providence had ordained should be brought to light wholly through his efforts. All that Camillo knew at first was that little Raffaello lived off in the country with a woman named Faustina, who was not in any way related to him. There was nothing remarkable in that; and Camillo would never have given the matter another thought, if Raffaello had not been such a handsome little fellow, in spite of his peasant clothes, and if Camillo had not remembered something that had happened in Florence, a few years past. The more he had seen of the child, the more he had become convinced that there was something to be found out about him. For that very reason, he was cautious, and had not questioned Raffaello too closely, but chosen, rather, to learn all that he wished to know, through some ingenious researches of his own. That was what he meant when he said he had been "studying ancient history."

In the two months that Raffaello had not seen him, Camillo's love of investigation had been plenti-

fully fed, and he had been very busy indeed, and
the chief subject of his business was little Raffaello.
The very next day after the boy's visit to Camillo
and the *madre*, the old *cocchiere* went to the Piazza
del Annunziata. It happened to be a saint's day,
and he stationed himself very near the portico of
the church, that he might see the great *signori* when
they came out. He had been there but a few minutes when a magnificent equipage drove up to the
church door, so close to Camillo's humble coach
that if he had not just then been so absorbed in his
own thoughts, he might have felt sensitive at the
contrast between his bony nag and his own shabby
appearance, and the spirited horses and gay-liveried
coachman and footman that sat with dignity on the
box of the splendid carriage. He noticed that there
was a crest engraved on silver fastenings close to the
horses' ears, and that there was something of the
kind on the doors of the grand equipage. He
immediately wheeled his own cab around, and took
a slow survey of the carriage on all sides, and then
brought his horse nose to nose with the aristocratic
thorough-breds. The crest on the door was the
same that Raffaello had described to him : a yellow
crown, and under it a large and fantastic B.

Camillo could scarcely suppress his agitation.

His big blue eyes were almost popping out of his
head; and his fat fingers clutched at his reins as
fiercely as if they were the threads that would un-
ravel the whole mystery.   Several people straggled
out of the church and made a beckoning motion to
Camillo, signifying that they would like the services
of his cab and horse; but he sat in blissful igno-
rance of them, with the air of one whose time is too
precious to be spent in considering common, ordi-
nary folk.

Presently, a white-haired old man and a tall and
beautiful young girl emerged from the church, and
stood a moment on the portico.   Camillo almost
jumped from his seat.   The young girl wore a pure
white dress, and her hair fell on her shoulders in
rich, dark waves; her eyes were large and soft; her
cheeks were delicately pink; and her mouth arched
at the corners into an angel's smile!

"A thousand maledictions on you!" ejaculated
the excited *cocchiere*, addressing himself vehemently,
"if you have n't seen those eyes before! Camillo,
you are not such a pumpkin as you look.   Where
have you seen them?   Never mind where.   A
cocchiere with a *madre* and a parrot to feed does
not spend his mornings hanging around in front of
church doors to see the angel *signorine* come out,

when there 's nothing more to be got by it than a
frost-bitten nose!   No, no, Camillo, you would
never have come here this morning, if you had not
had your suspicions, and, as usual, your suspicions
are correct.   And what of that! it 's a bad day for
foxes when Camillo is mistaken.   You 're as sharp
as any of them, even if you *are* a beggar of a
cocchiere with a face like a cooked lobster.   Santa
Catrina!   Look at those curls! where have you
seen them before?   Where, eh?   *Ecco*, may the
saints leave me in Purgatory, if I don't find out
something more from Mariotto!"

With that Camillo cracked his whip, and crossed
the *piazza* just as the great carriage, with the old
man and the lady, was turning into the Via della
Colonna; and he drove off at a mad pace, with never
so much as a customer in his cab, which he might
easily have had, if he had been attending strictly to
business, for it was a cold, rainy day.

Mariotto was the painter who lived on the floor
directly below Camillo and the *madre*, in the old
house behind the Church of the Badia.   He was a
young artist and a poor one, though his pictures
were very beautiful; but he had not yet a name,
alas! and few people bought any of them.   Nevertheless he painted day after day, week after week,

and month after month, and sometimes he would give away his pictures for the sake of getting people to notice them, in the hope of being recognized some day as a great artist. From him Camillo learned a great deal of what was going on in the city, and would often get bits of news about some of the great people. It was his habit to drop in at the artist's studio of an evening when business was dull, and crack a few Florentine jokes.

It happened to be on this very day, when Camillo had seen the *signorina* coming out of the Church of the Annunziata, that Mariotto, the painter, had received his order for the picture of an angel leading a little child. Mariotto was the happiest man in Florence that night. As he sat at his easel, sketching a variety of compositions for his great picture, and confiding his good fortune to Camillo, he was also making sketches in his own mind of the fame that would come to him if he succeeded in making it perfect. For the old *signor* who had given him the order was rich and powerful, and had promised Mariotto anything he wished if he painted the picture to please him.

Camillo took an unusual interest in the work, and watched it as it grew from day to day under the magic brush of the young artist. Often when he

had a minute to spare during the day, he would
step into the little studio, and chat with Mariotto
about the picture, asking all manner of questions
concerning it and the people who would own it;
and Mariotto told him all he knew. Camillo gave
his opinion of the work in his jovial way, and
cheered the young painter when he grew discouraged and despondent, as even great geniuses
are apt to feel sometimes, about their most glorious
work.

At last the angel was finished, and Camillo pro-
nounced it "most beautiful!" and it was perfect.
For Mariotto had painted it from the fair ideal of
his own imagination; but he was in despair about
the child. The child must be a human, living
creature that one must love from its very sem-
blance to other human children, and yet be lovelier
than them all. For that he must have a living,
human model, only adding to it the divine spark
of his genius that would make his work a master-
piece.

For days Mariotto hunted the streets of Florence,
hovels and public places alike, in search of a face
to put into his picture; and when he thought to
have found one, and had sketched it in beside that
of the angel, his soul grew sick and he would efface

it from his canvas, and then sit with his head in his hands for hours before it in mute despair. It was in such a mood that Camillo found him, one night, stopping on his way to his garret; and learning the cause of his distress, promised then and there to bring him a little boy who had a face that would go into any picture and glorify it. And that was the night on which Camillo had ridden so late to the little hut beyond the village of Galluzzo, and surprised Raffaello and Faustina out of their sad meditations.

CHAPTER X

RAFFAELLO had no notion of what Camillo meant by saying that the painter would make his fortune. The prospect of earning a bright silver *lira* to bring home to Faustina every day, and better than that, the pleasure of seeing his good friend Camillo whenever he went to sit for the painter, who lived in the same house with Camillo and the *madre*, was in itself a sufficient fortune for a little boy who wanted to be loved more than he wanted anything else in the world. On the morning after Camillo's visit, he was awakened very early by the crowing of a neighboring cock, and long before the cold gray morning had begun to break. It did not frighten him, as it once had done, to think of walking the long distance to Florence alone; for now he was a little older and much wiser, to his own thinking;

and he knew the road-way so well, and felt such a
nameless joy at the thought of being again in the
old gray city where the gentle *signorina* lived, that
he never minded the absence of the market-cart
and Pierrota, for his own legs were young and
strong, and served him better than the donkey's
would have done.   For, as the cold weather set in,
Pierrota had grown worse and worse, and so far
lost control of her donkey-temper as to kick violently at any one who came in her way.   It was
therefore considered wise by the members of
Luigi's family not to press her into service ; she
was declared out of health, and total rest and freedom for a time were prescribed for her, which left
Pierrota to wander about the village at her own
sweet will and fancy.   But those of the neighbors
who had felt the force of her iron hoofs, declared
that she was a lazy beast, and good for ten years
more of work, but had just got Satan into her legs.

However that might be, Raffaello had no need
of her services that morning.   He gained the Porta
Romana in good season, with the help of a good-
natured peasant who picked him up for the space
of half a mile or so on the way.

Florence was just the same as when he had seen
it last, only that it was colder and grayer, and that

the wind blew fiercely from over the ice-mountains,
and that the people were hurrying to and fro, hugging themselves together and covering their ears
and noses with their hands. Raffaello made his
way across the Arno and walked briskly to the

house where Camillo lived. The coachman was
already waiting for him, and led him straight to
Mariotto's working-room, where he pounded heavily
on the door and entered immediately after, without
waiting for his invitation.

"There he is!" exclaimed the *cocchiere,* as he

gently pushed Raffaello into the room, and unfas-
tened his scarf and cap. " This is the *bimbo !* Now,
take your spy-glass, my friend Mariotto, and search
the fields of Tuscany for a prettier one, and may
you turn into a leek if you find him ! " and he
raised Raffaello's chin, gazing at him admiringly,
and blinked and nodded with an air of immense
satisfaction at the painter.

As the little boy stood there before them, his
dark curls clustering about his neck, his eyes
widened with wonder and excitement, and the color
in his cheeks deepened with the crisp morning air
that had whipped up his young blood, he looked,
in truth, like a sweet picture of innocence and
youth. Mariotto drew back in astonishment, and
murmured under his breath, —

" *O ciel!* that is the face ! "

" Yes, yes, it's all very well to clasp your hands
and cry, ' *O ciel!* ' " put in the delighted *cocchiere.*
" It's just like you artists to sit and dream of a face
you would like to paint, and expect the Angel
Gabriel to drop one down from Paradise, and then
cry, ' *O ciel ! — Altro !* but it takes an old beggar
of a *cocchiere* like me to find you the very thing
you've been sighing for these three months ; and I
don't look much like the Angel Gabriel, either, do
I, Raffaellino ? "

Raffaello was not sufficiently well acquainted with that celestial personage to draw any compar-isons, but he slipped his hand into the coachman's, and said innocently, —

"I am sure you are just as good as the Angel Gabriel, Camillo, and I like you much better."

At which the *cocchiere* burst into a hearty laugh that seemed to leave an echo of his genial presence in the room long after he was gone.

Mariotto lost no time in getting to work after Camillo had left them, and he and his little model got on famously together, and were soon on very friendly terms. Raffaello found many things to interest him in the studio: there were many can-vases, in various stages of completion, standing about on the floor, propped up against the wall; and numberless sketches in pencil covering the sides of the room; there were several plaster and clay heads of grim old Romans with very dusty noses, looking down at him from high shelves; and odd bits of pottery, and old bronzes; and here and there some graceful flowers lifting their fresh heads out of dilapidated vases, — all of which showed that al-though Mariotto herself was poor, his mind was rich enough to see beauty in plain and humble things.

But the best of all was the large easel with the

unfinished painting, in which Raffaello was to be put. It was a lovely angel robed in blue and gold, stretching out one hand to lead the little child, and with the other pointing upwards. There was such a wealth of soft, rich color in the painting, and such a look of heavenly sweetness in the angel's eyes, that Raffaello, who, like all the children of Italy, loved everything that was beautiful, became at once all absorbed in the subject, and could not refrain from questioning Mariotto about it.

"What is the angel doing with the child?" inquired Raffaello, as the painter began to mix some colors on his palette.

"Why, the angel is taking care of the *bimbo*, the way all good angels do; as I am going to take care of you when I have made my fortune with painting your picture," replied Mariotto, who was in his happiest and most hopeful mood.

"How do you mean to take care of me? Do you mean that you will take me away from Faustina, to live with you?"

"Oh, no, no," said Mariotto, "not unless you want to be taken from Faustina. Who is Faustina?"

"She is my — my — I don't know what Faustina is," stammered Raffaello; "she has had me ever since I was a baby."

"She is my — my —   I don't know what Faustina is."

" Not your mother? "

" No," answered Raffaello.

" Nor grandmother? "

" No."

" Nor aunt, nor cousin ? " urged Mariotto.

" I think not. She told me that she had found me, and that I did n't really belong to her."

Mariotto stopped painting, and eyed the little fellow curiously.

" And does Camillo know that? " he inquired.

" No, Faustina only told me last night, and I did not see Camillo long enough this morning to tell him about it."

The painter gave a long, low whistle, and continued to mix colors without saying anything for some time.

"And that child that you are putting in the picture, do you think that he was lost too? " asked Raffaello, returning to his own thoughts, " and that the angel is going to take care of him always? "

" Yes, yes," returned the artist, " that is probably it. Somebody always takes care of little children who get lost."

" And do their parents ever find them again? "

" Sometimes."

" I wish that some lovely lady like the beautiful

signorina had found me instead of Faustina; not
that I don't like Faustina, for she is very good to
me.   But she does n't care very much for anybody,
and sometimes she is cross with the cat."

"Well, perhaps a beautiful *signorina* will come
and take care of you, and love you very much,
some day," said Mariotto, encouragingly, "that is, of
course, if you are a very good *bimbo*, and hold your
head very still, while I put in your eyebrows; for
you don't want your eyebrows to go all awry in
the picture, like this — " and he made a dreadful
grimace, like Mephistopheles, which caused a mutual
laugh.

Raffaello could not help thinking what very
pleasant people lived in the old house behind the
Badia.   It was a gray, dingy, dirty, tumble-down
old house to be sure, with narrow courts and
crooked steps and broken shutters; but that was
nothing.   Mariotto and Camillo and the *madre*, and
even the parrot, were all jovial, good-natured, and
happy, as if they lived in a grand palace; and they
were all kind to him.

The painter was not at all like Camillo.   He was
younger, and not so big or so broad, and his face
was not so red, and his laugh not so loud; but he
was a pleasant friend, like the coachman, called him

mignone, and seemed to be fond of him at once.
And he entertained him so well while he worked,
that Raffaello did not get so very tired, sitting still
and looking one way.   He began to hope he would
have to come often to sit for Mariotto, and was
moved to ask, —

"How long will it be before the picture is
finished?"

"Ah, that I cannot tell. 'Chi va piano, va sanno.'[1]
It may be a long time. You are not weary already?"

"Oh, no.   I hope it will be a long time, for I
want to come often and talk with you."

"That's my fine *bimbo!*" exclaimed the artist,
well pleased; and he stuck his brushes over his ear,
and stood aloof a few steps, viewing his rough
sketch critically.

"Perhaps this will be enough for to-day; we must
not get weary of each other too soon, for there is
the picture for Faustina to do when this is finished."

"Yes," said Raffaello, "she wants it very much.
She would rather have it than the silver *liras*."

"She shall have the *liras* and the picture too.
But you will come to me to-morrow, and then again
the next day; and after it will be Sunday, and we
shall rest on that day, and ask the good Lord to

---

[1] "He who goes slowly goes well."

help us to do our work well," said Mariotto, who had a pious soul, and whose art was his creed and his religion.

" Yes," said Raffaello, " I will remember."

" And now, a pleasant walk to you, my *bimbo*," said Mariotto, patting him on the cheek, "and a good fortune to you!"

And as the little boy left the artist's room, he felt as if Fortune had indeed taken him by the hand, and was leading him gently onward, and would never turn her back on him any more.

CHAPTER XI

IT was several weeks after Raffaello's first visit to Mariotto's work-room, when one morning he entered at the usual hour, and found the little studio empty. He had noticed, as he made his way through the narrow streets, that the whole city seemed to be in a commotion and excitement; that most of the shops were closed; and that flags bearing the Italian colors were set in the windows; and that the people were moving in great crowds in the direction of the river-bank, the great Lung Arno, which is the avenue of the rich and noble.

Raffaello sat down to wait for the painter's return, wondering what *festa* day it might be, and where Mariotto had gone; for it was already late, and there was no sign of his having been at work that morning. The paints and brushes were put away,

and the tall easel was in its corner, and the picture
on it was covered with a cloth, just as he had left it
on the Saturday evening before, for it was then
Monday. There were only the remains of Mariotto's
breakfast left scattered on a little table at the other
end of the room; and everything showed that work
had been given up for that day, evidently on account
of some great festivity. For the Florentine man or
woman is like a child, when it comes to gay sights
and glorious processions; and Mariotto was young,
and, next to his art, loved best to mingle in the
gayeties of his simple, light-hearted, sportive people.
Little Raffaello was just wondering whether he
should go or stay, for the painter did not make his
appearance, when he heard the jovial too-loo-rool
and the heavy tread of the *cocchiere* on the stairs.

" Ah, you are already here, pretty pigeon," cried
Camillo, opening the door. " How long have you
been waiting ? "

" Oh, a long time," replied Raffaello. " Mariotto
was gone when I came in. Do you know where he
is ? "

" Where ? " shouted Camillo. " *Ecco*, little man,
don't you know? don't you know where everybody
is going to-day; where I am going, and you too, if
you will come ? "

" No," answered Raffaello, in surprise.

" Ha, ha, I forgot that your country-folk at Galluzzo never know what is going on in the city ;
some of them don't even know which way the Arno
flows, Santa Catrina! Well, I will tell you, *bimbo
mio*, we are all going to see the grand procession."

" And will Mariotto not come back to paint to-
day ? " asked the little boy, a trifle disappointed.

" *Che, che !* it is a holiday ; a great *festa*, Raffaellino, and people cannot shut themselves up in a
garret to paint, when our beautiful young queen
comes all the way from Rome to show herself to us,
and to wish us a Good-day ! "

" The queen ! " cried Raffaello.

" The king and the queen and the little Prince
of Napoli,[1] who is no bigger than you, and — " he
added in a lower voice, turning his head around
and addressing the two brass buttons on the tail
of his coat — " not half so pretty ! And all the nobility will be there, in their fine carriages, and every
Florentine that has got a sensible eye or two in his
head, will come out to see the lovely Margherita."

" Oh," exclaimed Raffaello, clapping his hands
in delight, " and you will take me to the procession,
Camillo ? "

[1] Prince of Naples, the heir to the Italian crown.

" That is what I came here to do, for Mariotto has lost his head to-day, and will not be dragged from his place on the Ponte Alla Carraja until dark. He adores the beautiful queen as if she were the Holy Mother herself! "

" And he will not want me at all to-day ? "

" He has said so ; and left me to bring you when I came, while he went on ahead to choose the best place in the crowd, and save one for us near him."

Raffaello thought no more of his disappointment in the exciting prospect of witnessing a fine procession of great people, a thing he had never seen. So he gave his hand to Camillo, and they went down-stairs together, and climbing on the box of the coach, made their way as speedily as possible through the curious multitude, all flocking the same way.

The whole length of the Lung Arno was thronged with people stationed on both sides of the street, for that was the promenade chosen by the king and queen on leaving the Pitti Palace. It was a splendid sight, this long smooth avenue following the graceful curve of the river, and enlivened with the gay crowd; the gray palaces with their irregular roofs rising picturesquely out against the warm-tinted sky, their balconies and windows

and *loggias*[1] filled with brilliantly dressed ladies,
and their reflection in the limpid Arno opposite
smiling back at them ; gay-colored flags flying at
every peak and gable, in sign of welcome to the
young sovereigns. It was a joyous day for the
Florentines, for there is nothing they like so well
as the sight of pageantry and pomp. As Camillo
had said, not a soul in Florence would have thought
of missing it, and it really seemed as if the whole
city were come out to see the royal procession, and
pay tribute.

Camillo left his cab and horse around the corner
in the Borgo, and pushed his way through the
crowd with Raffaello. Their friend, the artist, was
already perched on one of the stone arms of the
bridge of Carraja, and beckoned to them to come
near. He had been waiting there three hours or
more to hold this splendid point of view, as indeed,
many other spectators had thought it little trouble
to do, for a glance and a smile from the lovely
queen.

Raffaello learned, from hearing Camillo and
the painter talking together, that the king and
queen were on their way to Venice, there to meet
some great foreign emperor; and that they would

[1] Covered gardens on the roofs of houses.

remain in Florence but one day. Great festivities
had been prepared for them, in consequence, by
the Florentine nobility, and every one who wore a
title or had a coronet on his crest, would surely be
following in the royal retinue that afternoon. It
seemed a long time waiting to little Raffaello, who
was hemmed in by the crowd of tall men and
women, and who was so small that the only view
that was anywhere on his level was a motley array
of boots and legs and arms, gesticulating enthusi-
astically, as their owners whiled away the time with
neighborly conversation. But he tried to be very
patient, and only questioned Camillo now and then
about the little prince, wondering whether he would
get a glimpse of him from his lowly, hidden place
in the big crowd.

Camillo, however, was taking care of that. When,
at last, the royal carriages were seen in the far
distance, turning out of the Ponte Vecchio, and
moving slowly between the masses of people, and
the joyous cry of "*Viva la Savoia!*"[1] went up with
a shout and was caught up and repeated and echoed
the whole length of the brilliant avenue, Camillo
suddenly caught Raffaello up in his arms and raised

[1] "Long live Savoy!" The house of Savoy, of which the present
king is a member.

him on his shoulder, from which exalted position
— for Camillo was so very tall — the little boy could
see over the tops of thousands of heads the ap-
proach of the regal equipages.

"Oh, look, look, Camillo!" cried he, in great
excitement, "do you see some people sitting very
high in a carriage, dressed all in red, and with
something bright shining at their belts! Do you
think they are the king and the queen?"

"Ha! Ha! You little country pigeon!" laughed
Camillo. "Do I think they are the king and the
queen! Bless my buttons! I should say not! They
are only the coachman and lackeys! For all their
fine red jackets and curly powdered-wigs, they are
no better *cocchieri* than your old Camillo. I could
sit up just as straight, and hold my head just as
stiff, and draw the reins on my handsome steeds
just as tight, if I were in their shoes. It is only the
difference of being coachman to the king and queen,
and coachman to the people, that's all;" for Camillo,
who had a horror of being outdone by anybody,
could not refrain from passing a little professional
criticism on those whom Fortune had placed a few
degrees higher up the scale than himself. "But
never fear; every onion has its own time for sprout-
ing, and mine may not be far off."

" Oh, I should love to see you driving a splendid
coach like that, Camillo. I am sure you would look
much finer than anybody," said Raffaello, admiringly, for he truly believed that his friend, the
coachman, was capable of filling any post of honor
that might be assigned to him. At this genuine
echo of his own sentiments, Camillo patted the two
small legs that hung about his neck, as a mark of
his approval.

" Now, you will see the queen and the little prince
sitting in their carriage, as soon as they get a little
nearer. There! you can see the king now, standing up with hat in hand and bowing to the people.
Look, look! there beside him is the lovely Margherita, smiling like an angel. Long live the queen!
and the little prince, too, is looking straight at you
and nodding. Wave your hat, Raffaello, and cheer!"
and the enthusiastic Camillo threw up his own cap
above the crowd, and joined in the loud acclamation
of " Long live the king! Long live the queen!
Long live Savoy!" while the gracious young mon-
archs bowed and smiled on every side, acknowledg-
ing the homage of their subjects.

It was a glorious sight, and one that thrilled
every heart present with love of country and loyalty
to his king. The people shouted and cheered and

" There! you can see the king now, with hat in hand."

waved flags and handkerchiefs, and some few wept for joy. It was a scene of fairy-land which many carried home with them, and dreamed of and remembered for many days after.

Following the royal coach, came a long line of other carriages of state, belonging to the dukes and princes of Florence, and to all the high families, ceremoniously arrayed to befit the great occasion. But the eyes of the crowd were following the red figures of the royal footmen as they towered high at the head of the procession, and finally disappeared beyond the tall gates of the Cascine.[1]

Suddenly little Raffaello, who had been watching with the rest, gave a quick start, and clutched very tightly at the patient Camillo's ears.

" See! " he cried under his breath, as he brought his little face close to the big one, " there she is! "

" Who? Where? " asked Camillo, showing no emotion.

" The beautiful *signorina*, my *signorina!* " whispered the little boy, in an agitated voice.

Camillo turned and beheld, among the last of the carriages in line, the one he had seen that morning, several months ago, in front of the Church of the

---

[1] A large park.

Annunziata, with the bright silver trappings, and the yellow coronet and monogram on the door.

"Surely! it is the Signorina Francesca!" exclaimed Mariotto, who was standing close to them.

"Do you know her?" asked Raffaello, eagerly.

"*Ecco!* who does not know the pretty creature? You see the people are looking at her now, as if she were a queen too. She is a queen among some of them; she is so kind to the poor, she helps them, and goes about to take care of them when they are sick. That is her old grandfather sitting next to her. Poor old man! It is the first time he has ridden out in public for six years!"

Mariotto went on talking with Camillo and one or two bystanders, about the Signorina Francesca; but Raffaello heard no more of what was said. He was intently watching the beautiful face that was turned smiling to those who knew her. Her soft, large eyes had a look of sadness in them. She glanced down at the crowds as if in search of some one; she did not look up so high as Camillo's shoulder, — she was looking at some young children that stood near the edge of the street. Once or twice Raffaello's little heart fluttered with the hope that her eyes would meet his, if only for a second; but they did not, and she was soon past. He felt a pang of disappointment, as if all the splendor of the great procession and the smile of the beautiful queen had suddenly been wiped out of his memory by the sudden apparition of this fairer vision which had so long been in his thoughts.

He looked a long time in silence after the vanishing figures of the old man and the young girl, not knowing why this sudden loneliness had come over him at the sight of her, and why he felt like laying his head on Camillo's neck and crying his heart out.

Camillo and the painter had stopped talking, and were standing waiting for the crowd to move, when some one laid a hand on the coachman's arm, and said in a hoarse whisper, —

"You have got him here in this crowd, perched upon your shoulder, for every soul in the city to gaze at! O Saints! Why did I ever let him come!" and looking down, Raffaello saw Faustina, with a frightened face, clutching at Camillo's arm.

"Ho, ho, Monna Faustina! you are too late for the procession," said the *cocchiere*, not one whit disturbed by the woman's agitation, as he landed Raffaello once more on his feet. "You should have made an earlier start, and come yourself with the *bimbo!*"

"What do I care for your processions!" she retorted angrily. "Will they give me back what I have lost? I did not come to see your silly parade, and your smirking hateful nobility, who are here to flaunt their riches and blessings in the face of poor wretches! I came to find my boy, when I heard that there was *festa*, and that you would all be flocking here, mad fools! to grin like apes at those who spit upon you!"

"Stop that bleating!" cried a bystander, who had caught the tone of Faustina's words and thought he scented a quarrel in the air.

"Brimstone!" shouted one or two others, gayly, relishing the prospect, "Look out for the explosion!"

But Camillo, who wished particularly to avoid any scene just then, patted Faustina soothingly on the back, and said good-humoredly, —

"There, there, dame Faustina, your *bimbo* is safe, and no one has been harmed; where is the use of making yourself any bad blood over it!"

Faustina made no reply, but gave her hand to Raffaello, saying nervously, —

"Come, let us hasten back to the village; it is growing late!" and she hurried away out of the crowd, like one afraid of being seen, never slackening her step or uttering another word until they were far out upon the country road, and the lights on the Arno were beginning to twinkle in the distance, and the sun was sunk deep below the purple mists of Carrara.

CHAPTER XII

A MONTH later, it was nearing the end of March, and the hills round about Galluzzo were already brilliant with the hues of returning spring. Faustina sat beside her hearth, preparing the evening meal, and Minnetto lay eying her with lazy interest, while Raffaello was gone to fetch a jug of fresh water from the spring near by. The door of the hut stood open, and Faustina was looking out upon the pretty landscape which stretched itself before her, with a sense of deep relief and a quietness of spirit which she had not known for many weeks.

Raffaello had stopped going to the city every day to sit for Mariotto, the painter, for now the picture was finished, and had been sent to its owner, and nothing had come of it. Raffaello was still with her; and the picture which Mariotto had painted

for her hung there on the wall, and the little
money-box in which they kept their treasures was
filled with bright silver pieces which the little boy
had earned. Fate seemed suddenly to have smiled
on them and prospered them, and Faustina began
to hope that Heaven would not punish her as she
deserved to be punished, by taking the child away
from her, — this gentle boy who had come to her
when she was in trouble and despair; who had
given her something to care for, to work for, and to
think of. She dared to hope that Providence had
sent him to her to keep, and to love always, and to
make a better, gentler woman of her. She was one
of those who are hardened and embittered by sorrow.
Her life had been a desolate one, but it had been so
through her own doing. Yet there were times
when the softer side of her nature rose to the surface, and she felt that she would give all she had to
show Raffaello how much she loved him; when
she longed to be kind and gentle with him, and
teach him so to care for her, that he should never
want to leave her for anyone else. She had been
afraid to do this, lest sometime the day would come
when they should have to be parted from one
another, and all her old sorrows should be renewed,
and his young heart grieved. But now, it was

nearly a year since he had first gone from the seclu-
sion of his earlier childhood, and had mingled with
other people, made friends, and grown familiar with
the big city; yet no one had guessed the truth, no
one had known him, he was still hers.   Ah, that is
what Faustina thought!

She had had many secret fears during that long
year just past. She had passed many sleepless nights
for thinking of the danger of his being recognized.
But so far, all her terrors had proved vain; and
to-night she was hopeful, and she determined hence-
forward to trust to Heaven's mercy for the only
sweet thing that was left in her life, and to show
the boy that he was her only comfort.

When he returned with the jug of water, she
drew him to her side, and, passing her arm around
him, said, —

"Kiss me, Raffaello!"

The child laid his head close to hers.

" I have not been a mother to you, Raffaello *mio*.
Heaven sent you to me long ago, to comfort me
when I was in great trouble, and I would not be
comforted. But now, if you will only love me
better than any one else in the world, I will be a
good mother to you; I will try to make you forget
that I have not always been kind."

" Camillo entered, and made his best bow."

Raffaello could not promise to love Faustina better than any one else; there was already some one who held that place in his young affections, — the beautiful Francesca, whom he had seen but twice, but whose image was always in his thoughts. Why was it that he could not love Faustina like that? since he had to live with her and be near her always. Why had she not made him love her before? But Faustina had not foreseen that the child's heart could not be turned of a sudden to her after those years of loneliness; and that for very need of the tender affection which he had lacked, all the ardor of his young soul was centred upon a fair vision whom he worshipped secretly as if she had been a being from another world.

As they stood there together in this near and new relation, Faustina hoping that all would be well, and Raffaello wondering why it was not, a dark shadow fell across the doorway, and made them both look up.

" Ah, it is you, *Sor cocchiere*," said Faustina, rising as Camillo entered and made his best bow to her, and gave his usual cheery greeting to the little boy.

" Yes," said he, sitting down and running Minnetto's tail between his fingers, " Camillo is like a

mushroom, he is always shooting up in the night-
time. Yet mushrooms, you know, make a good
sauce for men's meat, sometimes."

"You will make a good sauce to ours, if you will
stay and eat a morsel with us," said Faustina, who
was in a kinder mood, and who was beginning to
share everybody's opinion that Camillo was an
honest fellow, and the best of company.

"*Ecco!* Faustina, Camillo has never refused a
woman anything, and it would be late to begin now,
especially when he sniffs such things as *that* in the
neighborhood!" responded he, eying one of Faustina's round white cheeses on the table. " I was
on my way from leaving some visitors at Certosa,
and something in the wind — it must have been
the scent of your fine cookery — told me to step
in, and see how you and the *bimbo* fared."

"You have very good nostrils!" said Faustina,
laying another plate for the coachman.

"Ay, and very good luck, too, to find such favor
with the handsome *padrona!*" returned Camillo,
with great gallantry. For although he was only
a common coachman who drove a battered old
hackney-coach for a living, and who dwelt under
the roof of a tumble-down old city house, he had
that natural kindliness of heart, and genial spirit,

which made it impossible for him ever to have an enemy, and which attracted everybody to him, even so hard and unfriendly a person as Faustina.

He drew up his chair to the table when Faustina had brought out the provisions she had made for their supper, and he waxed so jovial and amusing, and praised Faustina and the neatness of her house and table so frankly, and was so gentle with Raffaello, and played such comical tricks with the cat, that he at once established himself as a friend of the family, and won Faustina's enduring regard.

Now, whatever it was that Camillo had in his mind, when he came to the little hut that evening, — whether it was really only to pay them a friendly call, or whether it was for a hidden purpose, — it would be very difficult to say. Camillo was such a sly old fellow that one could never quite guess his thoughts, except to feel certain that they were always honest and generous ones.

It chanced that during the course of the meal he grew so confidential, that Faustina was moved to talk a little about herself, — a thing she had not done in many years. She was in a softer mood that evening, and the big warm-hearted coachman, with his kindly face and genial ways and pleasant laugh, was just the person to draw out her sympathies, and make her feel that he, at least, was a friend whom she could trust.

"Benedictions on you, my good Faustina! you have, in truth, had your sackful of troubles!" exclaimed Camillo, with feeling, when she had spoken of the death of her husband and of her little boy, and of how she had been left alone and comfortless for many years; "but trouble is like the ice-wind from the Apennines, — it blows in at everybody's door, and chills every man's marrow; the rich man's as well as ours. We all have a taste of it, bless you! and it is an evil-tasting morsel whenever it comes."

"Ah, but some of us have it bitterer than the rest, friend Camillo. The rich man can keep many troubles from his door; and those he cannot keep wholly away, he can make easier to bear. Which is better, to have sickness and the loss of dear ones added to poverty and misery; or to have wealth and friends and comforts left to console you? Do not talk to me of trials being equal here below; the rich and the great have everything to make them forget their troubles; the poor have everything to make them remember."

"Not always so, Faustina. Sometimes the great

cannot forget their sorrows any better than we; they feel and suffer just like us. I have seen much of it in the city ; for there the hovel and the palace stand one next to the other, and one can see out- side one's own windows, and find that others have their burdens to bear. You who live in the coun- try, with no other neighbors than the birds and flowers, that are always happy, think yourself ill- used, indeed; but look about you in a city like Florence, and you will find thousands who would envy you. *Ecco !* I am thinking now, at this very moment, of a certain rich old man in Florence, who would give all he has, — his wealth, his fine lands, and his great name, everything, — to have this pretty *bimbo* here beside you !"

Faustina started, and looked at the coachman questioningly.

" Who ? " she asked.

" An old gentleman of the nobility who has known great misfortunes, when you talk of misfor- tunes and of losing dear ones."

" Lost children ? " inquired Faustina.

" Ay, children and grand-children," said Camillo, with a look that was full of mystery.

" All dead ? "

" Ah, worse than dead ! " returned Camillo.

"What do you mean?" demanded Faustina,
whose face had suddenly grown white, and wore
the old hard look. "What do you mean by worse
than dead?"

Camillo felt that he was getting very bold, and
wiped his face with his pocket-handkerchief before
replying, —

"Ah, friend, it is a long story, and a sad story;
I did not come here to talk of dismal things," and
he cast a glance at Raffaello, who sat listening intently to what was said. "Let me come and tell
it to you on the next penitential day, when you
need to shed a few tears for your sins, which I am
willing to wager a pair of rabbits' ears are not
worth the trouble of confessing!"

"No, tell it now," said Faustina. "You cannot
make me waste any tears over other people's
troubles. I have spent them all on my own."

CHAPTER XIII

THE coachman finished the bit of cheese that remained on his plate, and mopped his face again, for he was growing very warm with the prospect of his narrative. He leaned far back in his chair, pressing the tips of his fingers together, and gazed steadily at Faustina.

"Well, it happened the same year that the little Prince of Napoli was born. You remember that was in the winter, and the other took place just after the feast of the *Pasqua*,[1] six years ago."

"No, I do not remember," said Faustina, "anything that happened at Florence six years ago, for I was out of Florence then, and had just come here to live with Raffaello alone, and shut myself away from the rest of the world."

[1] Easter.

"*Ecco!* I remember it well enough. All Italy was full of it, and Florence talked of nothing else for two years. The old man had married his beautiful daughter to a young nobleman of very high family, and they often went to Rome, where she was greatly admired among the great folk on account of her beauty. The old *signor* was very proud of her, and would never hear of her staying away from any grand feast. They had two children: a little maid of ten, and a *bambino* of a boy, scarcely more than a year old. That year, just before the *Pasqua*, the young *signora* and her husband went to attend the baptism of the little prince at St. Peter's, and while they were gone the terrible thing happened."

Camillo paused a moment. The yellow flame in the fireplace flickered once or twice, and lighted up the room, so that he saw Faustina's face, still white, and intent upon him.

"It was spring, and the time when the people flock out to the beautiful Gardens of Boboli, on account of the flowers and the sunshine, and the pleasant company to be met with on a Thursday afternoon. The *bambino* had gone there with his nurse-maid, against the old *signor's* wishes, who would not allow his grandson to be seen in the crowd with the

common *popoli*. But the young wench had a lover
to meet, some good-for-nothing soldier, no doubt,
who paid her such violent court, and blubbered such
a pack of rubbish in her silly ears, that she forgot all
about her little boy, who had just learned to toddle,
and who was taking this opportunity to make use of
his little legs, and was running away from her.

" The last bells at sundown were ringing, and the
people were nearly all out of the Garden, before she
discovered that she had lost him."

Faustina rose from the table, as if she had been
struck, and walked to the little window where the
moonlight came streaming in, and stood there a
moment with her hand on her heart, and her face
turned away from Camillo. The good coachman
watched her closely. It was getting harder and
harder for him to proceed in his narrative ; his own
kind heart was very sore for her.

" Ah, Faustina, I see that I must stop; you are
beginning to be weary of my story," he said.

" No ; go on, now that you have begun. Tell it
all ! " she said, with a desperate ring to her words.

" Shall I go on, Raffaellino *mio?* " asked Camillo
of the little boy.

" Yes, yes, Camillo, tell us more about the *bambino*.
Was he really lost ? I want to hear it all," whis-

pered Raffaello, who was now standing close to
the old coachman, and was drinking in his every
word.

" Lost," repeated Camillo.

" And was he never found by anybody ? " asked
Raffaello.

" Santa Maria! They searched the gardens night
and day for a week, they dragged the fountains,
fearing he had fallen in, they scoured the city, and
dragged the Arno; the nurse-maid went crazy with
fright, and could never tell straight what had happened, and how he had slipped away from her.
The whole country was on the hunt; but never a
sign or a rag did they ever find of him, not even so
much as a little shoe, though some said he had
been gored by a mad bull that had just escaped
from Al Prato."

" Did they ever think he had been stolen ? " asked
Faustina, coming back to the table.

" At first, they thought it; but when they had
offered fortune after fortune to anyone who would
bring the child back, and no one ever came, they all
believed, like noodles that they were, that he had in
some way got into the river and been carried off to
the sea. That is the way with these Florentine
magistrates; everything they don't know what to do

with, they put into the Arno. *Grellotta!* how the men did stand and dispute about the matter, in the *piazzas* every day at noon! But disputing did no good, and the poor *bambinetto* was given up for drowned, and there were more masses said over the little innocent than would be needed to take a regiment of bad paste like me out of Purgatory. Then, the matter was forgotten by every one but the old *signor* and the young mother and father, and the pretty little *signorina*, who was just old enough to know she had lost her baby-brother."

"And when did they stop the search?" asked Faustina.

"Stop it? not till the father and mother were both in their graves, she with grieving, and he with having caught the fever searching like a madman down in the low countries near Napoli, that summer. Now there is no one left but the old *signor* and his grand-daughter; but though the one is an old man and the other a young girl, I think *their* hope is not quite dead. It is hard to believe death till we see it; and they are always hoping to find their little one. Ah, it is pitiful to see them always going to church in their splendid carriage, looking so broken-hearted in spite of their riches and their coronets! What comfort do you think riches bring to them,

when they think day and night, that the child of
their own flesh and blood is somewhere, perhaps,
in this big world. living in poverty and want, while
they are rich!"

Camillo looked very hard into Faustina's dark
eyes as he said this, and she looked back into his,
and the two remained silent until Camillo saw that
something glistened on the edge of her black lashes. .
Then he turned, and met Raffaello's face close to
his.

" It is my *signorina!* " whispered the child.

" Yes, it is the Signorina Francesca, whom you
saw praying at the Annunziata, and who was in the
queen's procession that day."

" Oh ! " exclaimed little Raffaello, clasping Camillo's hand more tightly.

" Now, Faustina," pursued the coachman, returning the little boy's caress, and making his voice as
gentle as he could, for he felt that he had ill-repaid
Faustina for her hospitality, " I have not told you
this to grieve you ; but I know that you women are
all tender-hearted, and that if you heard the story,
you could not refuse what I am going to ask."

" What can you ask of *me?* " groaned Faustina.
" Is it not I that am at your mercy ? Speak then."

" Not so, good friend, it is you who must grant

the favor. I leave it to your own heart whether you can refuse it or not."

Faustina made no reply. Her heart seemed to have stopped beating, and she was trembling, not so much with fear that Camillo knew the whole of her dismal story, but with a sense of wretchedness at the sudden flight of all the hopes she had cherished but a moment ago.

"Not long ago," continued Camillo, "the old *signor*, who thinks of nothing but his affliction, took a fancy that he would like to have a picture of a child resembling his little grandson. He hunted all the galleries of Florence, and had pictures brought to him from everywhere; but he found nothing until one day he chanced to see one of Mariotto's paintings, and admired it. Then he said to the Signorina Francesca, ' I will have that artist paint us a picture that will look like our child, a face with your eyes and your mother's smile.'

" The order was given to Mariotto for a picture of an angel leading a little child, and the old *signor* promised that if it pleased him, he would make Mariotto's fortune. When it was finished, and the old man saw the face of the child, he fell on his knees before it, and cried, ' That is like my son ! That is like Francesca ! Bring the child who bears

that face to me, and let me look upon him living.
No matter who he is, or where he comes from, I will
make a son of him, and he shall share my heart and
fortune with Francesca!'

"And now, Faustina," and Camillo lowered his
voice almost to a whisper, "is it not for you to say
whether Raffaello shall go to comfort the old man
who is broken in body and spirit, and who has suffered even more than you? I know that you are a
good woman, and that you will do what is right. If
you should choose to say he shall not go, and no
one should come to force you, and I should promise
to hold my tongue forever, you might perhaps keep
the child, for every one thinks the *bimbo* was
drowned in the Arno, you know. But think of
the sinfulness of it! You must speak from your
heart."

It was a terrible moment for Faustina, who
had never cared for others' sorrows, and who was
now called upon to give up, of her own free will, the
one precious thing of her life for another's happiness! No wonder she wavered between right to
the child and right to herself, after her long years of
hard feeling and revengeful bitterness. She had
always said to herself, when her conscience troubled
her sorely, "I have not stolen the child. He came

to me!" Then, she knew nothing of him; but now, if she kept him in spite of everything, it would be stealing him; he would suspect her, and she would never win his love! Her hard hands were clenched and her teeth were set. She felt desperate and ready to do any mad thing, until she felt Camillo's hand touch hers, and his kind voice whispered in her ear, —

"Courage, Faustina, the Holy Madonna will help you!"

The contact with that generous upright nature, the sympathy expressed in his tones and touch, turned the tide of Faustina's feelings. She held out her hands to the little boy.

"Come here, Raffaello *mio*," and she folded him in her arms. "You are that little child. That old man is your grandfather!"

Raffaello uttered a cry, and threw both his arms about her neck.

"You came to me in the Gardens that night, and I brought you here to live with me, because I had lost my own little son; and I tried to believe it was God that sent you to me. Now you have found your kindred, and you must go to them. They are rich and powerful; they will make you very happy. Only forgive me, Raffaello, for having kept you from them so long, and try to think kindly of poor Faustina!" and she laid her face against his, and wept again.

"Dear, dear Faustina!" cried the child, suddenly finding that he loved her very much now, and trying to comfort her. "Don't feel sorry, please. You have been so good to me; I shall never forget you; and I want you to be happy too!"

"*Brava! brava!*" cried Camillo, who felt that they had been dismal long enough, and who never felt at ease in a dull atmosphere. "Everybody will be happy to-morrow; and there will be *festa* and rejoicing all over the city; and dame Faustina will be made a duchess, or some such fine thing, for having found the baby Barborello, and saved him from the jaws of that mad bull. *Hola !* Alleluia!" and he tossed up his glazed hat, which had been put on the floor beside him, with such a flourish, that Minnetto, who had been taking a nap in the crown of it, took such a sommersault as he had not had for many a day; and then retired to the back of Faustina's chair with an injured expression, and in evident disapproval of such familiarity.

CHAPTER XIV

NEVER had the world looked so bright and the day so joyous to little Raffaello, as it did on the following morning, when he and Camillo made their way, hand in hand, up the steep road that stretched northward beyond the Porta San Gallo.   Behind them the city lay nestling close together in the broad, beautiful valley, with its cathedral and palace towers gilded red with the first touch of early sunlight, and the Arno curling its silvery way between the gray stones, and Galileo's Tower rising on the opposite slope, from out the rich new growth of vineyards and olive-orchards and budding mulberries.   Before them rose the most fertile side of the great Apennines, mantled with young fields and hoary cypresses, and studded here and there with pretty villas and flowered terraces; and higher still, fair

Fiesole lying like a gem on the bosom of the green mountain.

Raffaello, being a child of Tuscany, with an inborn love for all that is beautiful, would have carried a glad heart that morning, amid this surrounding loveliness, even if he had had no other reason for being happy. But the great mystery of his childhood had at last been solved. All that he had sought so long to understand, was now made clear, and his greatest childish hope was fulfilled. He would live always with the beautiful *signorina;* she was his sister; she would be fond of him, and never look sad again, and he would have the right to love her dearly. Raffaello never lost the remembrance of that early silent walk, when, with his hand in Camillo's warm grasp, his heart gladdened by his familiar friends, the wild myrtle and the arbutus, whose scent filled the air, he turned his back forever on all his childish loneliness and longings, and went forward to meet a new life of happiness!

Camillo doubtless felt as much as Raffaello, if not more, that morning; for he was silent, and that was very unusual with him. As he went panting and puffing up the steep mountain-road, growing redder at every step, he was thinking of poor Faustina, sitting alone in her hut, and of what a

hard thing it must have been for her to give up the
little boy whom she had loved and reared from his
babyhood; and he was wondering, too, with a secret
chuckle, if there was not a way in which he might
console Faustina, and make her loss easier to bear.
Faustina was a fine woman, there was no question
as to that, Camillo thought. She had proved it by
the way she had given up the *bimbo ;* and now he
must look about him for some means of keeping
her from being too lonely.

But Faustina, sitting alone with her cat that
morning, was not so disconsolate as Camillo supposed. To her own surprise, there was no bitterness in the thought that Raffaello was gone from
her, to be with those who would cherish him and
make him happy. She had often looked forward to
that time with terror; yet, now that it was come,
and through her own consent, she felt that blessed
peace, the consciousness of having done right, which
is ever the reward of an unselfish deed. She had
prayed humbly and penitently for the first time in
many years; and her prayers had been heard. She
was comforted and almost happy, far happier than
she had ever been when her whole heart and mind
had been intent upon avenging herself of her bitter
fate. Raffaello had promised to make her happy,

and never to forget her. He had a noble generous nature. Perhaps he would love her more because she had suffered for his sake. When they, his people, learned that she had received him when he came to her to fill the gap in her own broken heart, perhaps they would not think so ill of her, and would let him be kind to her. They were rich and great, she was lowly and poor, and they might pity her. She was no longer proud and resentful. She had learned that such feelings bring no joy to any one. She had learned of the simple, large-hearted Camillo that the only way to be truly happy is to think much for others and little for self.

When Raffaello and his companion had climbed nearly half-way up the road which leads from Florence to Fiesole, they stopped in front of a tall gateway, fancifully wrought in iron, and hung from two huge pillars surmounted with gryphons. The gardens were enclosed with high stone walls that hid from the passer-by all the loveliness within. But Raffaello, through the open fret-work of the big gate, caught glimpses of a beautiful villa rising high among the trees, and of a winding, flowered walk leading up to it; of fair white statues and sparkling fountains, dotting the bright green terrace.

" Is this the place ? " inquired Raffaello, timidly.

" This is the villa Barborello ! "

"This is the villa Barborello!" returned Camillo, trying to assume an air of unlimited confidence, but in reality feeling a trifle nervous and abashed at his proximity to all this magnificence. He pulled out his pocket-handkerchief, and wiped his face several times, and then brushed the dust from Raffaello's boots and his own, and coughed very loud and unnecessarily once or twice, before making up his mind to put his hand to the bell.

Before he had time to ring, the tall iron gate swung open, and they saw the grand carriage with the old *signor* and the lovely Francesca sitting in it, just appearing down the winding drive-way. Camillo was surprised into immediate action. Stepping forward as the horses were nearing the gate, he doffed his shiny hat, saying, with an air of grave importance, —

"A thousand pardons, your excellence! a word with you and the fair *signorina!*"

Seeing the child with Camillo, the old nobleman ordered his coachman to stop, a triumph which caused the old street-*cocchiere* to tingle with gratification. That such a stiff-necked, silver-buttoned, powdered-wigged individual as the Barborello coachman should be ordered to stop for him! With growing courage, he approached the carriage-door, and said, presenting Raffaello, —

"This is the *bimbo* that Mariotto painted in your picture. With your excellency's and the *signorina's* permission, I have brought him here."

"Ah, let me see this little man whose face was good enough to be put in Mariotto's picture," said the old gentleman, getting out of the carriage, and taking Raffaello's face between his hands.

"It is not only his face that is handsome, your worship!" exclaimed Camillo, greatly encouraged by this reception. "Let your nobleness but look at his legs! as fine and straight as a little prince's! There are not many such among our common people, else my name is not Camillo!"

The *signorina* smiled and held out her hand to Raffaello, and he went to her as naturally as a flower turns to a sunbeam. He was too full of happiness to utter any words. She led the way to a rustic seat under some trees, at a distance, in the garden. The old man watched them both attentively.

"He is wonderfully like Francesca! wonderfully like her; the dark curling hair, the lustrous eyes, the upward turning of the lips! Truly, Mariotto's picture is perfect!"

Camillo stood at a respectful distance, his hands behind his back, ogling and blinking alternately, and burning to be more closely questioned. But the old *signor* was absorbed in studying Raffaello's face, and seemed to have forgotten the presence of the *cocchiere*. He remained silent, till his eyes rested on something that hung and glistened around the little boy's neck.

"What is that?" he exclaimed, starting suddenly, and laying his trembling hand on the gold-linked chain and the small round medal that Faustina had taken out of the locked box and placed round Raffaello's neck that morning before he left her. It bore the face of the Virgin on one side, and the yellow coronet of the house of Barborello on the other; another medal like it hung on Francesca's breast.

"It is our lost child! O Holy Saints, our little Nino returned to us, after these years of waiting and praying! Tell me, good man," he added, turning to Camillo, "tell me if it is so; whether it is I who have lost my senses!"

Francesca hastened to soothe the old man, who stood white and trembling at the discovery, and laid her hand gently on his forehead, whispering, —

"Dear grandfather, I am sure it is our little one come back to us. I know it by the love I feel for him. Listen, and this kind friend will tell

us all he knows about it, will you not, good Camillo?"
and she turned to the coachman with a pleading
smile.

"O *signorina mia!*" cried Camillo, 'I would
tell you all I know and more too, if it took me the
next minute to Purgatory, to see that look in your
sweet face! I am only a poor *cocchiere* who lives
in a garret with his old *madre*, and does not meet
with the gentility face to face every day. But as
sure as I am standing before you, I said, the first
time I ever saw that *bambino* in the Piazza Santa
Maria del Fiori,[1] 'There's a little pigeon fallen
out of its nest!' and the next time I saw him
buying gay beads for Faustina at the *mercato*, I
said, 'I'll go in search of the parent birds, no
matter how high they fly!'"

And then Camillo told, in the finest language
he could command, how with cautious and secret
investigation he had learned more and more of
the little fellow; of his lonely life with Faustina
and the mystery that seemed to hang about him;
and remembering the loss of a child in a great
family, some years ago, and making note of
Raffaello's beauty and fine features, and his resem-
blance to the beautiful *signorina*, which he had seen

[1] The Cathedral Square.

"It is our lost child! O holy saints!"

at a glance that day at the Church of the Annunziata, he was satisfied that the whole mystery was
in his keeping. Then he related how he had been
to see Faustina and drawn her story from her, and
the confession that Raffaello was the child who was
lost long ago in the Gardens of Boboli. He told
how she herself was suffering and desperate then,
and how the little helpless thing, toddling towards
her with its arms outstretched and clutching at her
dress, seemed to have been sent to her from
Heaven ; and how she had prayed to be forgiven for
having caused others to sorrow; how she had
striven to do right by the boy, and loved him as
much as it was left in her heart to love any thing
or creature.

Camillo's recital was very touching, for he could
be as pathetic at times as he was droll, and he
felt deeply for poor Faustina. The old man was
moved with compassion. He had no thought of
being angry, or of punishing the woman who had
taken Raffaello when he had come to her unbidden,
and cared for him, and saved him, perhaps, from
worse ills than that of falling to the shelter of a
humble widow's hut. He was too grateful, and had
suffered too long in patience, to cherish any other
feeling than that of joy at the strange recovery of

his little grandson, and the mysterious answering of his prayers.

He held the child's hand in his, as if afraid of losing him again, and every now and then looked into the young face with an expression of doubt.

" Tell me, Francesca, that I am not dreaming," he said, turning to the fair *signorina*. " Tell me that our lost one is found, and that we three, on earth, shall part no more!"

" *Fratello mio*,"[1] said Francesca, sweetly, " speak to our father; tell him that you will never leave us!"

Raffaello laid his cheek close to the old man's.

" Yes, I will always stay with you," said he. " You are my grandfather, and she, the beautiful *signorina*, is my sister. Faustina has said so, and Faustina knows better than any one, does she not, Camillo?"

" Surely, your sweet excellence," responded Camillo, suddenly realizing the grandeur of Raffaello's position, and never lacking in respect.

" It will make me very happy to live with you here, in this beautiful home. But we must not forget Faustina. She must be made happy too. She has been good to me, and worked for me, and I have promised never to forget her."

[1] My brother.

"She has been good to you?" asked the *signor*.

"Oh, yes, but she was very unhappy sometimes, because we were so terribly poor, and she could not give me everything she wanted. But I think she is very fond of me."

"She shall never be poor again!" said the old nobleman, rising. "Francesca, Raffaello, my children, give me each a hand, and let us return together to our home. And you, good Camillo, take my coach at the gate, and ride as fast as my horses will take you to fetch Faustina. You shall all have your reward."

There was an affectionate parting between Camillo and the little heir of Barborello, which seemed in no way out of place to any one but the coachman and the footman, still in dignified waiting at the gate. Then the three walked slowly toward the villa, while the honored *cocchiere* bounded into the aristocratic carriage with the ease and air of a prince, and gave his orders to the "canary-colored legs," as he called them, feeling that this was, indeed, the most glorious hour of his coachman's career.

CHAPTER XV

IT was not many hours before the whole city of Florence was thrown into a tumult of joyous excitement at the news that the little son of the great house of Barborello had been brought back to the home of his parents by a certain lucky *cocchiere*, who for some reason, seemed to take the whole credit of the matter to himself. Camillo sprang into immediate prominence, and his name was on every tongue, as if he had been the most important person in the whole affair. Like all great and conspicuous personages, he had often to meet with many envious and sour remarks, from the mouths of those who had been less shrewd than he. For weeks after, he could not ride through the city on the top of his brand-new coach, cracking his whip in the air in his usual jocose spirit, without hearing all around him cries of: "*Ola!* there he goes, there goes the gentleman *cocchiere*, who holds *festa* with the nobility! Ha, ha, ha, where's your other hat, Camillo? Come, come, boys, light your pipes at the end of his nose!"

But Camillo was in too good a humor, and too well satisfied with himself, to take offence at their silly jests. He would only crack his whip the harder over their heads and shout, "*Via, via*, you pack of sour crabs!"

In truth, Camillo's star of good fortune seemed to be shining very brightly now, and he could scarcely contain his happiness at the successful issue of his great scheme. There were the old *signor* and the pretty *signorina* and little Raffaello, all three living together at the grand villa, as happy as any one could wish; and there were Faustina and he and the *madre*, and Minnetto and the parrot, actually making one family, and in possession not only of the hut, enlarged and embellished into a veritable little villa, which was the envy of all the neighbors at Galluzzo, but also of a large and flourishing garden around it, with grape-vines and fig-trees all their own; every bit of it the gift of the old *signor*, who had followed Raffaello's wish that Faustina should be made happy.

Camillo, not wishing to be backward in this mat-

ter, at once endeavored to persuade Faustina that
she could not live alone any more, and that he was
the only person in the world who could rightly protect her, and make Raffaello's absence bearable, because of the interest and love they both had for the
little fellow. And as Faustina had already learned
to admire the good Camillo, and had seen the folly
of shutting herself away from the many kind souls
there are in the world, she made little objection.

She soon found that, after all, life could be made
very pleasant, when people were kind and thoughtful toward one another, and laid aside their own
troubles. For Camillo, who had been a good, duti-
ful son, proved a no less kind and faithful husband,
and he and Faustina lived very peaceably and contentedly together for the remainder of their days.

But I really cannot say as much for Minnetto and
the parrot, who, I grieve to record, led a life of
mutual misunderstanding and strife; for Coco very
soon evinced a wicked fondness for tweaking poor
Minnetto's tail, whenever the old cat lay snoozing
comfortably in some favorite corner. Minnetto was
not accustomed to tail-pulling; he never had been
accustomed to it, and to change his habits, at his
time of life, was asking too much. Whenever Coco
grew too unbearably familiar, Minnetto would quietly

retire to some inaccessible spot on the chimney, or on a cornice in the wall, and from there look down with disdain upon the enemy; while Coco would strut up and down the room in fine rage, his eye cocked on one side, trying to lure Minnetto back with his finest flow of parrot-language.

But it was not only Camillo and Faustina who were made happy by the change in little Raffaello's fortunes. Not one of his old friends was forgotten, and each one, in some way, had a share of

his bounty. Luigi and his brothers received a handsome new market-cart and a fine young donkey of a most amiable disposition, to take old Pierrota's place. Even Giojoso's stall was supplied each spring with fresh vegetables from the rich gardens of the Barborello ; and as they cost him nothing, his profits grew very large, so that he was soon able to retire from business.

And Mariotto, the young artist, was set up in a
beautiful new studio, with plenty of models and
canvases, and the beautiful things he loved to have
around him. He painted many pictures that were
hung and admired in the Academy, and he grew
rich and famous very fast.

As for little Raffaello himself, I think he was
the happiest of them all; to feel that all those who
had been his friends were now made happy through
him; to be so loved by the old *signor* and the lovely
Francesca; to know that with them he had a home
which held blessings he had so long missed, was
reward enough and happiness enough for him.

For how sweet is the happiness, dear children,
that comes to us after we have known trouble!
How much more do we appreciate blessings for
having felt the lack of them; how grateful do we
learn to be for every good thing that comes into
our lives when we have been taught its true worth
by suffering! And ought not we to believe that
the trials that come to us in this world are sent for
a purpose to our good; and that if we bear them
dutifully and in patience, we may see the good of
their teaching even in this world; that it is only
God's own wise and merciful way of dealing with
us?

I think that little Raffaello's joy in being restored to the dear ones he had lost so long, was
in no way lessened for having spent those lonely,
almost sad years of his childhood in Faustina's
humble home. Those years had taught him a great .
lesson, and moulded his young nature for gentleness
and mercy. He was rich, and in time he grew to
be powerful; but in his greatness he never forgot
the people, the dear, simple, humble people whom
he had known and loved; and he never ceased to
work for their good, because he, himself, had been
one of them.

THE END.